The Mystery of the Moonlight Murder

An early adventure of
JOHN DIEFENBAKER

By Roderick Benn

This book is fiction but many of the characters and events are based on real people and actual historical events.

Text © 2009 Roderick Benns

For an Access Copyright license, visit www.accesscopyright.ca
or call (toll-free) 1-800-893-5777.

ISBN 978-0-9812433-0-6 (pbk.)
ISBN 978-0-9812433-1-3

$12.95 CDN.

Library and Archives Canada Cataloguing in Publication

Benns, Roderick, 1970-
   The mystery of the moonlight murder : an early adventure of Prime
Minister John Diefenbaker / by Roderick Benns.

Includes bibliographical references.
ISBN 978-0-9812433-0-6

1. Diefenbaker, John G., 1895-1979--Childhood and youth--Juvenile
fiction. 2. Prairie Provinces--History--1905-1945--Juvenile fiction.
3. Prime ministers--Canada--Juvenile fiction. I. Title.

PS8603.E5598M98 2009   jC813'.6   C2009-903715-7

Cover, book design and illustrations by riad

ACKNOWLEDGEMENTS

I would like to acknowledge the assistance of the Diefenbaker Canada Centre and in particular Rob Paul, who was unfailingly helpful in my requests.

For Canada, its leaders and the legacies they left behind.

For Canadians, who in their wisdom and diversity chose them.

For young Prime Ministers in waiting, who may one day give of themselves to their nation.

— Roderick Benns

For my wonderful wife, Joli, whose love and unwavering support had made this project possible.

Thank you for being my first editor, life partner and friend.

— Roderick

For Eric and Ali, my children. Thank you for enriching my life. May each of you listen to your heart and follow your path.

— Dad

"I do not care what language a man speaks, or what religion he professes, if he is honest and law-abiding, if he will go on that land and make a living for himself and his family, he is a desirable settler for the Dominion of Canada ..."

Clifford Sifton
Minister of the Interior,
House of Commons in July 1899

Contents

The author uses the term 'Indian' in this book, rather than 'First Nations' or 'Aboriginal' person. It is what a First Nations person was called at the time of this story. The author and publisher discussed what term to use in the story since 'Indian' is outdated and its use is in decline. Great effort was made to be historically accurate throughout this book and so we decided to use 'Indian' only to help put the reader in the time period of this story.

The reader will note that the tone of the book, through the characters and plot development, is meant to acknowledge the historical wrongs made against First Nations people and to support their important legacy. It is the author's hope that once parents, teachers, and children read this book they will have a greater understanding of the challenges faced by First Nations people in Canada a century ago.

Summer, 1908

On the prairies,
near Borden, Saskatchewan

Central Saskatchewan, Canada

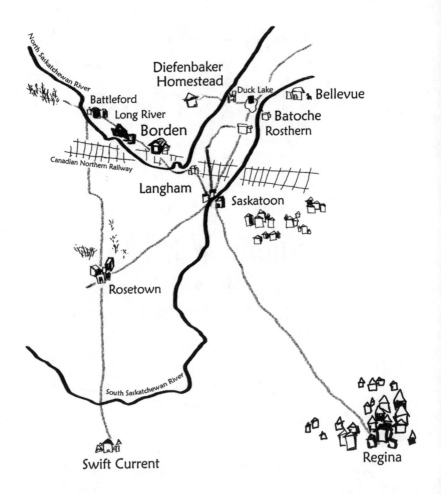

North Saskatchewan River

Diefenbaker
Homestead

Duck Lake

Bellevue

Battleford

Long River

Borden

Batoche

Rosthern

Canadian Northern Railway

Langham

Saskatoon

Rosetown

South Saskatchewan River

Swift Current

Regina

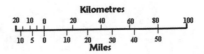

Kilometres

20 10 0   20   40   60   80   100

10   5 0   10   20   30   40   50

Miles

Chapter 1

The Killing Field

John Diefenbaker couldn't have known that his neighbour had only twenty-two more seconds to live.

His younger brother, Elmer, had finally stopped his nearly-endless chitchat about a quarter of a mile back. As they rode their horses along the well-worn prairie trail, John knew that this wouldn't necessarily last, so he enjoyed the silence while he could. A full moon shone across the endless Saskatchewan prairie, while green Northern Lights danced ablaze in the summer darkness. It was a night to remember.

Sixteen seconds.

The Diefenbaker family had run out of water unexpectedly after a small fire erupted in the kitchen. With their well not working properly, getting water meant going to the river a few miles away or bartering with a neighbour. The boys' father, William, sent them to the Petersen farm a mile and a half up the road. Old bachelor Petersen was always willing to trade his water for some of Mary Diefenbaker's home cooking.

John and Elmer had bundled up a supply of breads, butter, and a large tub of rabbit stew to trade for the water. They had tied it to Elmer's bronco, old Blue, for the journey to Karl's and now the same horse carried containers of water tied to saddlebags for the trip back home. John's horse didn't have a saddle, since the Diefenbakers could only afford one and John was a strong enough rider to ride bareback. Soon they would be past the Schneider farm and nearly home.

"John?"

"Yes, Elmer?" John knew the silence couldn't have lasted much longer.

"Remember that time we built the wooden wagon and tied Mother's parasol to the back, thinking we could fly it off the second floor of the barn, like the Wright brothers?

Eleven seconds.

"Of course I do. Remember how we almost killed Tip by making him the pilot? It was foolish, Elmer. We almost killed our dog! I'm twelve and you're ten now. Anyway, that was two years ago. We were just kids."

Four seconds.

"Yes, but do you think it would have worked if the dog had been smaller?" Elmer asked, as if that had been the single flaw in the plan.

John sighed.

"Elmer, it never …"

BANG! The sound of a gunshot shattered the stillness and was followed by a rasping scream. John's horse jerked up onto its hind legs and tossed him from its back like a rag doll. He still held onto the reins but hit the ground hard with a grunt. At the same time Elmer's horse bolted, aiming its nose toward home with Elmer gasping and holding on for dear life.

John looked up just in time to see a shadowy figure scurry into a dense grove of poplar trees far off in the distance behind the Schneider farm. The Northern Lights continued their dance as John achingly got up, his heart racing. He wanted to shout out toward his younger brother who appeared smaller and smaller as Blue carried him down the road at breakneck pace. But it was obvious that Elmer was long gone, thanks to the survival instincts of Blue. John only hoped that his brother was able to hold on until he got home—and that the water got there, too.

John, his heart still pounding, climbed back onto Skipper now that the horse had calmed down. He wasn't sure whether to head in the direction of the gunshot or his house. After pausing briefly, John decided to proceed toward the sound, convincing himself that Mr. Schneider had shot at a coyote, which was going after his chickens. But then why did he hear someone cry out? Wasn't it the sound of a man in pain? As his mind raced to make sense of what had just happened, he saw a figure on foot fleeing the tiny farm house and racing toward the

fence line. A woman's scream pierced his ears, which was followed by a sustained whimpering as John bolted toward the
sounds.

"Oh my Lord! Hans! Hans!"

Mrs. Schneider was now in view as John rushed his horse to
the scene. He found her cradling her husband in her arms,
sobbing uncontrollably. There was blood on her hands and
clothing as she hugged Hans Schneider close to her.

He wasn't moving.

"Mrs. Schneider…is Mr. Schneider…is he…" John began.

She looked up briefly and stared mournfully into John's eyes
and then the sound of her cries carried across the prairie fields.

It was a night John would never, ever forget.

Chapter 2

The Rebellion

"About how far away were you from the place where Mr. Schneider was shot, son?"

John looked away from the Royal North West Mounted Police officer's eyes as he searched for the right measurement in his mind.

"I'd say we were about five hundred feet away, sir, Elmer and me," said John quietly. Elmer nodded affirmatively, though he was unsure of his brother's estimation skills.

In the background, John's mother, Mary, busied herself in the tiny, three-room homestead. She was making coffee for the two officers, who were clad in their trademark red uniforms. They had arrived early to piece together the events of the night before. John's father, William, sat near the officers. Elmer and John were both on the floor, cross legged. John's uncle, Ed

Diefenbaker, stood in the home's single doorway, his lean frame half in and half out. There just wasn't room in the cramped, tiny kitchen for so many people. Like many settlers in the area, the Diefenbakers earned enough to get by but not much more, and their home's size reflected this.

"And Gertrude Schneider tells us that you saw something," Sergeant English continued. He was the lead investigator, a man William and Ed had gotten to know somewhat, and he looked every bit his forty-five years. The heavy lines around his forehead suggested someone who had seen all sides of prairie life.

"She thinks maybe you got a look at who did this?"

John swallowed. Normally he was excited when officers from Borden, the closest town to the Diefenbaker homestead, stopped by to chat while on their patrols. But this was anything but normal. This was the day after their neighbour, Mr. Schneider, had been shot.

"It was dark, Sergeant. I didn't see anything except a shape running off. Everything happened so fast."

"What kind of shape?" Constable Wood joined in. At twenty-four, the constable was obviously the junior partner. He was tall and athletic looking, with short reddish hair.

"It was the shape of a man, sir," said John haltingly. "I fell off my horse when he reared up and as I sat up and looked in the direction of the gun shot, all I could see was a figure. It looked like a man, but I couldn't tell you more than that."

John wished he could. He prided himself on his excellent memory and attention to detail. Even in school his Uncle Ed, who was also his teacher, marveled at John's ability to recall facts and dates, especially when he had to defend a point he was making.

"Wasn't there a full moon last night?" pressed Sergeant English in his deep voice. "And I remember seeing the Northern Lights fired up when I stood outside the station. Are you sure you couldn't make out anything else, with all that extra light?"

John felt like he was letting them down. "There were a lot of shadows, sir. Maybe he was tall, but I couldn't tell anything else. He moved pretty fast."

"Tall," repeated Sergeant English while he wrote it down in his notebook.

"Tall and moved fast." Then he looked over at his partner. "That could have been you out there, Constable Wood," he said with a wry look.

"Except for the fact that I was trying to get some sleep," said the young officer, who looked slightly irked at his partner's attempt at a joke.

Ignoring this, Sergeant English took his coffee from Mary with thanks, his large hands smothering the hot mug. Constable Wood did the same.

"Well, we know old Hans was outside working in the moonlight," said Sergeant English. "That man wouldn't have known how to slow down if you paid him to. But what were you two young pups doing out that late anyway, if I might ask?"

John's father, who was a thin and hollow-cheeked man, very much like his brother Ed, cleared his throat.

"I sent them to fetch water from the Petersen farm. The well's been acting up again and we ran out after we had a small kitchen fire. I knew the boys could handle it. They're both good riders. Of course, who would have thought anything terrible like this was going on?" William asked.

Sensing his discomfort, Mary placed her hand on his shoulder. The sergeant nodded.

"I'm sure they're fine riders," he said, nodding to the boys, as John and Elmer sat up straighter. "It's not every day horses hear gun shots around here, let alone at night," Sergeant English added. "It's normal they'd get spooked."

"Tell me," said Sergeant English, continuing, "what do you know about River's Voice?"

William looked puzzled.

"He's a member of the Cree Indians, the band just west of here. We've known him for three years, ever since we've been in the Borden area. He stops in from time to time to do some trades and he usually leaves his daughter, Summer Storm, with us while he travels around. She's almost like a sister to the boys. I'd consider him a good friend."

"What does he like to trade?" asked Constable Wood.

"Usually rabbit and venison. In return he likes milk, eggs, and butter for his family," said William. "Always fair trades, if you ask me. We also throw in some apples from time to time, since my brother in Ontario, Duncan, often sends a few barrels of them," he said, gesturing to the corner of the cramped homestead where they stood.

"Apparently you aren't the only one he tries to trade with," said Constable Wood.

"Oh?" said William.

"He's also paid a couple of visits to your neighbour, Hans, in the past."

William shifted uncomfortably. "Well, like I said, he makes his rounds. It makes sense. There are quite a few farms around here that might be interested in what he has. It's not always easy for farmers to get meat, especially when most of us are working dairy cows."

John and Elmer glanced at each other, wondering what the sergeant was getting at.

"Well, Hans Schneider wasn't interested. Apparently they were having words," said Constable Wood.

William stared at the officers.

"Surely you don't think River's Voice had anything…" began William.

"We're not thinking anything at all at this point," Sergeant

English interrupted. "In fact, everyone knows Hans Schneider had words with pretty much everybody. He was a heavy drinker. Easy to set him off. It seemed to be the nature of the man to make enemies, that's for sure."

He smoothed his thick, sandy moustache.

"You know, this area has been pretty quiet around here in the last few years and that's the way we like it. We've thrown a couple of whisky smugglers out of town before, and rumour has it there's another one or two pushing his luck. Like I said, it's no secret Hans himself wasn't above hoarding a few bottles."

Mary shook her head. "Land sakes," she muttered under her breath. If there was one thing Mary Diefenbaker didn't appreciate, it was alcohol.

"So, other than a couple of suspected whisky smugglers in the area," Sergeant English went on, "it's been pretty quiet. Of course, it wasn't that long ago when we used to hear gun shots all the time. And we don't want those times to return."

"What gun shots? What times?" Elmer piped up.

His father looked irritated. "He means the rebellion. And I hope you remember at least some of this, considering we covered it last year."

William was Elmer's teacher, although school was out for the summer. John went to school in a different district with his Uncle Ed each day. With two teachers in the family, there was always a heavy expectation on learning.

Ed was nodding in agreement. "Both of you should have at least some idea what the sergeant is talking about."

"We know about the rebellion," said John, taking care to defend his brother, too. "It was in 1885."

The sergeant nodded and looked thoughtful. "That's right. And this being 1908, I guess I was… what?… about twenty-two or twenty-three years old? Pretty much the same age as Constable Wood over here," he said, nodding to his younger partner. "And I was one of about five hundred men sent to Battleford, once things began. We had already lost three good officers. We didn't want to lose any more."

"You were in the rebellion?" asked John excitedly.

"Tell us more!" said Elmer eagerly.

"Elmer Diefenbaker!" said his mother, embarrassed by his request.

"It's fine, it's fine," said Sergeant English, who was as close to smiling as ever today. "Kids love to hear a good story and this one's as true as the day is long. It's one thing to learn about it in school and another to hear about it from someone who was really there."

He took a sip of his coffee before he continued.

"Well, you know how it all started. This area was all part of the Northwest Territories just three years ago, not Saskatchewan as it is now. The Métis leader, Louis Riel and his military general, Gabriel Dumont, led a revolt against the federal government for all kinds of reasons."

John had studied a great deal about the challenges of the Indians and Métis, who were half Indian and half European, mostly French. They weren't treated fairly by the federal government. Their land was handed out to settlers from the east. Worse, commercial hunters hunted their main source of food, the buffalo, almost to extinction. The federal government's response was to encourage the Indians and Métis to switch to farming. But the change was too hard and they were still living near starvation.

The Northwest Rebellion happened because the Indians and Métis grew more desperate. Riel and Dumont had a list of demands that they wanted answered for their people.

Ed spoke up to prod John's memory.

"You'll recall Riel tried to form alliances with the Cree Indians and even the white settlers," said Ed. "Many of the settlers were ticked off that the railroad was built so far south from where they were living. He brought anyone on board who would help him take on the federal government."

Sergeant English nodded his agreement.

"My uncle says Gabriel Dumont was one of the best fighters in the West," said John. "We've met him, you know."

Ed gave an awkward smile.

"Is that so?" said Sergeant English, raising an eyebrow

dramatically. "I think your uncle's right. Mr. Dumont was indeed an exceptional soldier for the Métis. I thought I had heard he visited you from time to time, back when you lived in Carlton."

There was a slight accusatory tone in the sergeant's voice.

William bristled. "Yes, and the Royal North West Mounted Police would visit us too. We've always opened our doors to everyone," said William defensively. "You know that."

"Yes. Too bad Dumont was on the wrong side of the law," the sergeant said.

There was a tense silence before the sergeant continued.

"Like I said, there were about five hundred of us and we marched up from Swift Current to Battleford to try and stop the raids. First we got the news from Duck Lake that nine civilians and three officers had been killed in March by Dumont and Indian rebels. Then we got word Chief Poundmaker had a bunch of his men on the move, ready to attack.

"But Chief Poundmaker just wanted to talk, didn't he?" pressed John. "He even sent a message ahead of him to say so. His tribe was hungry and they were angry that the government wasn't helping them, like they had promised," said John, always ready to defend the underdog.

John's mother looked like she was about to say something, but the sergeant caught her eye as if to say "Let it go."

"I can't say things were perfect for the Indians," replied Sergeant English, "but everyone was struggling. Most everyone's still struggling." He paused, as if attempting to figure out how to best tell his story.

"You see, some of the Indians had begun to break into farm houses. They carted away supplies from the general stores, killed cattle and took folks' horses. Now I have to admit, the Cree pretty much returned to their reservation. They had left Battleford before our force arrived. But some of them weren't innocent and they continued to loot the towns. A few days later, we marched west up the Battle River in pursuit of the Cree, near their own camp."

"The battle of Cut Knife Hill," said William quietly.

"Exactly. I have to admit, they counter-attacked fairly well. We were ordered out of there."

John squirmed in his seat and looked at his father, who seemed to read his son's mind.

"And Chief Poundmaker gave the order not to give chase to the officers," William added calmly. "Isn't that right, Sergeant?"

The sergeant looked annoyed, while John felt proud that his father had spoken up. From what John had understood Chief Poundmaker had never wanted to fight.

"Anyway," said Sergeant English. "Poundmaker's dead now. So is Dumont. Or at least I thought he was."

Ed scrunched his forehead. "Dumont is dead. He died two years ago. Everyone knows that."

Sergeant English frowned and nodded. "I know it. But there's a new problem, and it's one that's bringing back a lot of bad memories for me. There's someone new in town, a young man who apparently just stepped off the train two weeks ago from Winnipeg. He's been stirring up the Métis and some of the Indian tribes. Even some of the settlers around Borden. He's got a powerful way with words and he's already starting to gain a following.

"What does that have to do with Gabriel Dumont?" asked William.

"He's André Dumont, Gabriel Dumont's nephew," the sergeant revealed. "And I've got a feeling he wants to finish off what his uncle started."

Chapter 3

The Rawleigh's Man

There was nothing but moon and stars, layered by a blanket of darkness. A man paced back and forth beside a small tent.

"He's dead? What do you mean he's dead?" the man asked in anger and disbelief.

Another man, sitting on a large rock, looked sullen.

"He surprised me. I didn't expect him there, out in the fields like that. It just kind of... went off," the sitting man answered. "When he already saw me, I didn't want to let him see my face."

The man stopped his pacing for a moment and thought, listening for any noises above the sound of crickets. He removed his hat and ran his fingers through his hair, something he always did during times of high stress.

"So you shot him. Now are there children in this family left behind? Will there be any children left alone because of what you've done?

The man on the rock shook his head. "No, he was old, remember? And they didn't have kids. What's gotten into you?"

The other man hesitated, and drew a deep breath. "You were there for one simple reason," he stated, stopping to stare at the man who sat still on a large rock. "And now everything has gotten out of control."

"I didn't mean to. Look, what's wrong with you?" the man on the rock demanded.

The standing man glared. "I have an important path, one I should have taken long ago. Now tell me, did you at least finish what you started to do?"

The man on the rock nodded.

"Good."

And with that the standing man swung his leg over his horse and looked down. He was about to say something else but instead simply nodded and rode down the trail, leaving the other man to brood under the waning moon.

***

William stood after milking the family's two cows and stretched his stiff back. He walked to the barn doorway with Tip, the black and white family dog. Morning had just started to break across the Saskatchewan sky and it was a time of day he rarely missed seeing.

It felt good to be healthy, William decided, which only someone who had been terribly ill could understand. After serious bouts of tuberculosis in Ontario, a doctor recommended the dry air of the prairies to calm his respiratory problems down. Once he got to Saskatchewan, all those breathing problems had gone away. He was a different man here.

John, who was piling wood in preparation for winter, now three months away, and Elmer, who was feeding the chickens, both stopped to watch the morning unfold, too. Soft daylight began to flood across the prairie, turning light bronze wheat fields into blankets of golden crimson. In a few weeks, the swaying wheat would be harvested. Selling the crop would make the months of hard work pay off—at least, if they could get a good price.

"Elmer Diefenbaker!" Mary was standing in the doorway. She had obviously been admiring the sunrise, too, but was also watching the way Elmer—his face turned up to the sky—was absent-mindedly pouring chicken grain all over his feet.

"If you can't watch what you're doing, I can find another job for you. And I can guarantee that it won't be as pleasant as this one," she warned sternly, implying that an extra turn cleaning out the cow paddocks was on Elmer's horizon if he wasn't careful.

"Sorry, Mother," Elmer replied, doing his best to spread the small mountain of chicken grain more evenly around the yard. The chickens swarmed around him, their heads jerking forward and back.

"And when you're done with that," she called out again, "you can help your brother stack wood. If we work on it a little bit each day we might just survive the winter."

Mary Diefenbaker liked to make everything a high stakes game. Life was all about surviving and it certainly wasn't a game of chance or a game for fools. Life was about being prepared and it was as simple as that.

William, on the other hand, had a bit of the dreamer in him. It was the other part of the reason that had led them to board the train west to Saskatchewan in the first place, aside from drier air for his lungs. This was far from the civilized roads and tall buildings of Ontario and into the empty nothingness the Canadian government liked to call 'The Last Best West.' It was where idealists, like William, believed small paradises might be found. Mind you, because of the terrible conditions of the train ride, half way there he wanted to turn around and go back.

But Mary wouldn't hear of it. You don't start something and then not finish it, no matter how hard things get.

People like William Diefenbaker had the courage to go west. People like Mary Diefenbaker had the courage to stay. Somewhere in between, couples like this completed each other across the empty stretches of land and made the West what it was—a dream that could only unfold one field at a time.

As Ed returned from the north field, where he had just finished mending a hole in the fence, John saw him disappear into his tiny one-room house built on an adjoining quarter section of land south of his brother's. Uncle Ed had his own place but everyone generally ate supper together. It was at his uncle's house where John slept, too, since the three-room homestead was so cramped with the rest of the family. In fact, Elmer had to sleep in the kitchen each night. Although there was no doubt that the Diefenbakers were poor, they worked the two quarter sections of land as a team and survived by sticking together.

William joined his boys at the woodpile, taking in the work that had so far been done. The high puff of dark hair on his head moved up and down as he walked. John noticed his father looked like he was lost in thought.

"Do you remember when we first found this land?" William asked them.

"Hard to believe," he continued, "that it was three years ago. At one point, all we had was a stake in the ground. Section Eight, Township 418. That's what was printed on it, remember? That's all we had. And now look what we've done," he declared proudly, his hand sweeping across the sprawling landscape.

John scratched his thick, wavy black hair and looked at the small thatched-roof barn where a handful of pigs snuffled the ground outside. The chicken coop, where Elmer had busied himself earlier, was alive with the sounds of clucking and grain-eating hens. He saw their own modest house, which was the centre of their lives, especially in winter. And then there was the land itself. The fields, once torn as the rich dark earth was overturned, were now bursting with wheat that would soon be ready to harvest. John knew his father was hoping for fairer wheat prices this year from the big grain companies. The family worked so hard for the money they earned.

All across the Canadian prairies, the stories of homesteaders were stories of the countries of the world. For instance, although the Diefenbakers were originally German, they had been in Canada for a while. But the Schneiders next door only arrived from Germany six years ago. Other homesteaders in the province arrived from Norway, Sweden, Ukraine, Russia, Poland, England, France, and Italy. And some were from other Canadian provinces and the United States where both white and black settlers had moved to take advantage of free land from the government.

"We've done a lot of work, Father," John had to admit. "We're lucky, aren't we?"

"We sure are," his father agreed quietly, and then he immediately looked wistful.

"You know, I don't know if I said this to you boys earlier, what with everything going on, but I'm real happy you're both safe. John, that was a lot for you to see…a lot for you to deal with. But Mrs. Schneider was sure thankful you were there with Skipper."

John nodded. He was glad that he and Elmer had taught

themselves to ride bareback. Their father had never gotten the hang of it and their mother was never interested. John and Elmer were both lean, which the horses probably appreciated, although John was a bit stockier than his younger brother. John's dark, tight wavy hair contrasted with Elmer's brown, straight hair.

John had to admit the image of Hans Schneider just lying there, dead, was not something he could shake from his mind. He stacked four logs of wood neatly onto the pile as his mind raced backward to the events after he had found Gertrude Schneider cradling her dying husband in her arms. John had stayed only an extra moment and then rode Skipper as hard and fast as he could back home to let his father, mother, and uncle know, as Mrs. Schneider had asked. William left Mary with a loaded shotgun, and then ran to be with Gertrude. Mary barricaded the only door to the homestead with the wooden hutch just in case the shooter came to the Diefenbaker farm. Meanwhile, Uncle Ed quickly hitched up the horse team and travelled straight to the police station to report the tragedy.

Now two days later, it was time to bury Hans Schneider on his farm, in a hole that neighbours, including William, had earlier helped dig. Gertrude Schneider was now a widow, with no children to help her.

"Who do you think did it, Father?" asked John. "Who would do such a thing to Mr. Schneider?"

William shook his head and watched the sun inch higher in its daily pact with the sky.

"I don't know, son. If I knew, I would have told Sergeant English yesterday. It doesn't make any sense to me," he added.

"But you don't think it was Summer's father, right?" John pressed.

"Of course not. That doesn't make any sense either," his father answered quickly, reaching over to straighten a corner of the wood pile.

John was happy to hear that his father still believed in the innocence of River's Voice. It was a special day whenever he visited and brought Summer with him, who was eleven, just a year younger than John. It felt like they had grown up together, even though it had only been about three years. Summer would often help John do his chores. This provided an endless source of fascination for her, seeing what was involved in feeding pigs, cows, and chickens. Although her family had done some farming on the reservation where she lived, it had not been very successful. Instead, her father did a great deal of trapping in neighbouring woods in order to provide for them.

"What do you think River's Voice and Mr. Schneider were arguing about, Father?" asked John.

"That's not for us to worry about, John. It's not our concern."

John wanted to say maybe it was because Mr. Schneider just didn't like Indians, but he kept his mouth quiet. But the fact was

John had overheard things. Like, when Mr. Schneider was complaining about other people to Uncle Ed or his father, especially about the Plains Cree Indians who lived in the area. He noticed his father would deflect any comments and just try to stick with topics that they could agree on. On the other hand, Mr. Schneider had been such a good neighbour to the Diefenbakers—helping them with the farm, being there if they needed anything. To John, it was strange that Mr. Schneider, an immigrant himself from Germany, had not been more tolerant of peoples' differences.

William took another glance at the work his boys were doing and then began to walk back to the house.

"You boys finish your chores and then go get cleaned up. The service is at eleven this morning."

***

The short journey to the Schneider house was a silent affair in the Diefenbaker Schooner. That's how everyone referred to their carriage. William and Ed's brother Henry, a mechanic now living in Waukegan, Illinois, had modified their wagon by adding a canvas roof and two coal heaters inside. Then he had installed stovepipes rising several inches above the roof of the wagons. Winters were especially dangerous on the prairies. After John and his Uncle Ed nearly froze to death in a blizzard last winter, the family didn't want to take any chances.

Of course, it's not as if the heaters needed to be on right now.

William and Mary, dressed in their only church clothes, were already starting to break out into a sweat as the hot morning sun, so strong in August, beat down. It was only ten o'clock and the temperature was already eighty degrees Fahrenheit. They all stared straight ahead, lost in the circumstances that had brought them to their neighbour's home.

"There's a storm brewing," Mary stated, breaking the silence. Pointing to the western horizon she added, "It'll hit tomorrow."

"That works out well. I'm going into Borden today to get supplies," William commented.

Although William couldn't see anything himself, he trusted his wife's instincts. She had always been the best weather vane he had ever laid eyes on.

In the back of the covered wagon, Ed was quiet, staring off at the wisps of clouds scattered about the sky. John and Elmer relived the evening of two nights ago in their minds, although Elmer's memory was of an awfully fast horse ride. Blue sure could go when the spirit moved him. John's mind kept flashing to the shadowy outline that had scurried into the forest and to poor Mr. Schneider, still as can be, in the arms of his distraught wife. He wondered if he should have given chase to the mysterious figure.

No one deserved what happened to Hans Schneider,

thought John. It's just not fair.

As the Diefenbaker wagon pulled up onto the long Schneider laneway, John fixed his intense, dark eyes on those who had already arrived. He saw about twelve people standing near Mrs. Schneider and recognized mostly everyone, including Pastor Mackenzie, who would be conducting the service. The boys frowned as they noticed the rectangular hole in the ground a few yards away with a mound of dirt beside it. John held his breath momentarily as he looked for signs of the body. He was certain that it must be in the wooden box under the large tarp he could see sitting on wooden slats.

As the Diefenbakers got out of the carriage and began solemnly shaking hands with the others, John noticed that many pairs of eyes were fixated on him. He felt self-conscious but tried not to show it, staying in step with his parents and uncle who were making the rounds of saying hello to everyone. He could feel a trickle of sweat beading up on his scalp.

Elmer nudged him. "Everyone's staring at you, John," he whispered. "You're famous."

John hit him back, in the way brothers do. "I am not famous, Elmer. They're just curious about what happened," he countered, feeling very awkward.

A few of the conversations seemed to be focused on Hans Schneider's love of "the bottle," as most of them called it. John knew that this meant whisky and alcohol in general. He didn't know why some adults drank alcohol, but his mother believed that it was a serious sin.

When another wagon, very different from the others, turned off the main trail and onto the lane that led to the farm house, it drew everyone's gaze. The boys felt their stomachs flip in excitement. *Mr. Wright!*

The carriage, drawn by two large quarter horses, was spacious and canary yellow. It had fancy black and gold script writing on both sides of the wagon, which read:

Earl T. Wright

The Rawleigh's Man

Quality Products

Kitchen needs, spices, medicines and miscellaneous

"I didn't know Earl would be here today," murmured someone, smiling.

"But it makes sense," voiced another. "Gertrude likely bought half the man's liniment stock, as much as old Hans used to complain about his back."

Earl T. Wright was probably the most welcome man in the Saskatoon-Borden-Battleford corridor. It wasn't that he was well known—he had only been on the job for a few months. But the Rawleigh name carried a great deal of weight when it came to getting quality products delivered right to your door.

As the area salesman for the respected company, Earl Wright was treated like an old friend, almost everywhere he went. A Rawleigh's man was a peddler who had anything one needed— salves for colds and cuts, spices for cooking from exotic places like China and the West Indies, and even beauty creams for those rich city women who had time and money for such luxuries. Not to mention, he was the best source of news one could ask for, since he travelled so much.

He had moved up from Montana a short time ago, carving out a new life for himself on the Canadian prairies where there was less competition and more elbow room. Almost everyone who came into contact with Earl walked away believing that he had just put their needs ahead of his own. But there were a few folks who didn't like him because he would never take anything in trade, just money.

As he stepped off the carriage, his prominent silver hair glinted from below his black formal hat. He had an equally-silver moustache. It twitched slightly as he surveyed the people in front of him with the perfect mix of concern and seriousness.

His deep-set blue eyes, although grim as the occasion called for, still contained his trademark twinkle.

John and Elmer started to run toward him. The slightly crushing hands on their shoulders belonging to their father and mother reminded them to slow their pace to a more dignified brisk walk.

"Mr. Wright! We didn't know you would be here," called John, with Elmer right on his heels. John and Elmer would often keep the Rawleigh's man in conversation for as long as the salesman would let them, or, more likely, until their mother told them to quit talking his ear off.

Mr. Wright smiled warmly as the boys approached.

"It's good to see you boys. I wish it were under different circumstances. That's what we always say at funerals, isn't it?"

"We don't know," responded Elmer truthfully. "We've never been to one before."

Earl patted Elmer and John on their shoulders understandingly as he made the rounds greeting the other adults. When one woman suggested making a purchase from him, he admitted that he didn't really feel comfortable engaging in sales before Hans Schneider was even buried.

"Let's meet after he's buried," he whispered. Neither the living nor the dead prevented Earl T. Wright from making a sale, and today would be no different.

After he conveyed his condolences to Gertrude, Earl walked over to where the Diefenbakers were standing and greeted William, Mary, and Ed. He liked the Diefenbakers for many reasons. More than once, Mary Diefenbaker had ordered some of Earl's home remedies for the cuts and bruises that unavoidably happen during farm life. They weren't his highest paying customers, but they were good ones. After all, times were tough for travelling salesmen, too. Earl always appreciated how the Diefenbakers exercised hospitality during his travels in their vicinity. The fact that William and Ed were both school teachers was appealing for Earl, too. It gave him a chance to talk about politics and the general state of the world with people who shared those interests.

"I heard how your boys got mixed up in all of this," said Earl to William and Mary. "I was sure glad to hear that they were alright. I don't know what's happening to this place anymore," he added, shaking his head. "I like the Schneiders. Like them a lot."

John and Elmer strained to hear the conversations from the grown-ups.

"The boys were fortunate, that's for sure," agreed William. "We all were, except for Hans."

After a somber silence, William continued. "They'll catch him, you know. They always do."

Earl nodded. "You bet they will. Probably some drifter, looking for a few dollars or something to steal."

"Nothing was stolen though, from what we've heard," countered Ed.

"Maybe he didn't get the chance," Earl suggested. "With old Hans out there working at night, well, who would have expected that?"

William looked slightly surprised. "How did you know he

was outside working?"

Earl brushed the comment aside. "Oh, heard from someone in Borden. You know how these things get around."

William nodded. "Doesn't take long, does it? Say, Earl, do you happen to know anything about Gabriel Dumont's nephew being in town? Sergeant English was telling us about him. I never heard of him before."

Earl leaned toward the adults, lowering his voice. John and Elmer leaned slightly, too, although they tried not to be obvious about it.

"I've seen him. And I don't like this fellow one bit," Earl admitted. "He's much too smooth, too charming, if you ask me. You get the feeling that he'd sell his mother if the price was right."

The Diefenbakers couldn't help but chuckle at Earl's description of the man. John wondered if Earl had any idea that people might think the same thing about Earl himself.

"What's he up to?" asked Ed. "Is he looking to farm?"

Earl snorted. "Farm! That boy knows as much about farming as I do. Together we wouldn't know a plough from a cow, I can tell you that much."

Everyone laughed quietly.

"No, he's just an agitator," Earl concluded.

"In what way?" asked Mary.

"He's trying to stir things up, like the old days here, from what the locals tell me. I saw him in Borden a few days ago. He's maybe all of twenty-four or twenty-five years old, standing on the back of a wagon like he was something. He was talking to five or six Métis men about how terrible the Canadian government is to them. They seemed to agree with Dumont's reasoning, standing there in awe, nodding their heads in agreement like trained dogs."

"Well, I have to say Earl, I wish the government would do more for the Métis and the Indians," said William. "The West has been flooded in the last ten years with homesteaders just like us from all over the world and it's changed everything for the Indians and Métis."

"True enough, and right you are. But putting the anger in people like this, getting them all fired up, well, that's just asking for trouble," Earl reasoned.

William thought about this for a moment. "Sounds to me like he may be related to Dumont but he talks more like Louis Riel," he said, "organizing his people and others across the West to stand up to the federal government and demand their rights."

"Could be a dangerous combination," stated Ed.

John and Elmer looked at each other and didn't say anything.

The boys tried to picture a man who was a blood relative of the military commander Gabriel Dumont yet who had the magnetic personality of Louis Riel whom they had read about. Dumont had evaded capture by fleeing to the United States once the 1885 Northwest Rebellion had been crushed by the Royal North West Mounted Police. He returned only when the government offered him amnesty, which means he was pardoned for leading the rebellion. Then, he led a quiet life until he died of heart failure at age sixty-nine. But Louis Riel didn't have that kind of luck. He was hanged in the same year of the rebellion for treason.

"My dear friends, I invite you to gather round," Pastor Mackenzie announced from beside the hole in the ground. He first talked quietly with the six men who had agreed to help lower Hans Schneider's body into the grave, to make sure that they were ready when the time came for their participation.

As people were taking their places, a red-eyed Gertrude Schneider thanked the Diefenbakers for coming in her thick, German accent. She had not learned a great deal of English while she had been in Canada, mainly because she was isolated on the sprawling, prairie farm. Not to mention, she wasn't a highly social person and this had made it difficult for Gertrude to learn the language.

"Hans always enjoyed you as neighbours," Gertrude shared with the Diefenbaker family. "And thank you, Earl," she added to the salesman, as he removed his hat and once again wore his extremely serious look.

"I should tell you the police came by this morning," she continued in an almost whisper. "They are going to make an arrest, you know. This news, you may not like it, but it's the truth," Gertrude uttered cryptically.

"Who are they going to arrest?" asked William.

Gertrude was just about to reply when the pastor began the funeral service.

"Ladies and Gentlemen, thank you for joining me here today on this sad occasion, to honour the passing of Hans Schneider,"

Pastor Mackenzie spoke in the same type of voice John was used to hearing in church.

"I can speak to you after," whispered Gertrude, quickly moving to her place beside the pastor. She wiped both sides of her face with her hands, bracing herself for the grief that would wash over her at any moment.

John and Elmer, who had overheard, wondered about this news. The police sure had done their job quickly.

"Please join me in the singing of *All in Jesus*," invited the pastor.

The group began singing as one somber voice, the notes hanging in the brilliant cloudless blue sky. As John's eyes glazed over, he imagined that he could see a moving shape in the open fields on the horizon. The eyes sometimes play tricks on the open prairies, even during the day. However, as the seconds went by, John realized that the shape really was growing. He bumped Elmer who nodded, having also noticed the dark-coloured dot increasing in size. John soon realized it was a human figure on horseback coming towards them. Given the angle and where they were standing, no one else could see or at least seemed to notice the movement in the fields.

John focused in and soon figured out it was the shape of someone young on the horse—a girl. Her long braided hair bounced up and down on the shoulders of her deerskin jacket as she rode toward them. John realized it had to be Summer Storm!

Chapter 4

Truth and Consequences

John motioned to Summer in a restrained way so that the adults wouldn't see, as if to say "Stay back." He was hoping that she would understand. Summer didn't disappoint, quickly steering her horse behind a large woodshed, out of sight.

If there were two things that Summer was good at—and there were many things, actually—they were hiding and hunting. John flashed back to last spring, when Summer tried to teach him and Elmer how to catch a rabbit with their bare hands. At one point, John and Elmer had collided in mid-air when they both leaped to catch a rabbit at the same time. The rabbit had escaped their clumsy attempts easily, but Summer made it look almost effortless. She had donated her catch to the Diefenbaker family, which had been a nice surprise for dinner that night. So far, the boys had never come close to mastering the technique.

After the assembly sang two more songs, Pastor Mackenzie spoke a few kind words about Hans Schneider. Six men then took hold of the handles on the sides of the wooden box and lowered it into the ground. Gertrude and some other women wept. Next, the men worked quickly to shovel the pile of dirt back into the hole. John felt uneasy observing the ritual as he looked for the right moment to go over and find out what Summer wanted.

Pastor Mackenzie thanked everyone for coming. His final blessing on the gathered people signalled that the funeral was now over. He offered final condolences to Gertrude then blended in with the crowd to chat. Meanwhile, William, Mary, and Ed struck up conversations with other neighbours. John and Elmer took the opportunity to move quickly in the direction of where Summer was hiding with her horse. When she saw them coming she sprinted toward them, her long, lean frame covering the distance quickly. She was the same height as John, even though she was one year younger.

"Summer, what are you doing here?" John asked as they drew nearer.

"They have my father, John! My father!" she panted, tears staining her face. John asked her to slow down because with her heavy accent, it was difficult for him to follow if she spoke too fast.

"Who? Who has your father?" asked John.

Summer took a deep breath in between sobs. "The police."

"They arrested my father. They said he killed him, but that's not true!"

John and Elmer gasped. John glanced behind him, where he could see his father, mother, uncle and Gertrude talking, all of them moving their arms in animated debate. Earl had moved away from the group, standing a few feet away. He was engaged in conversation with someone else, although he kept looking from time to time at the group having the lively discussion. Then Mary noticed where John and Elmer were and nudged William as she pointed at her boys.

"We're going to find out what's going on, Summer," promised John quietly. "This must be a mistake."

"A big one," agreed Elmer.

"John? All of you come here," called William, who was also moving toward them.

John, Elmer, and Summer began to walk toward them, Summer moving slowly and reluctantly when she saw Gertrude. It was Gertrude who spoke first.

"I want you to go!" Her face was contorted into bitterness as she stared at Summer.

"Summer and her father are friends of ours, Gertrude," William stated strongly. "You know that. This all has to be a mistake."

"No, no mistake," replied Gertrude plainly. "This girl," she claimed, pointing to Summer, "her father said to my Hans that my Hans stole his pelts! Can you imagine? He said this when he was in Borden, a week ago. Hans told me."

Gertrude was emotional again, now reliving the conversation. Her heavy German accent meant everyone had to be patient to understand what she was saying, as was common with many families who had arrived from different countries to settle on the prairies.

"Pelts? You mean animal skins?" asked John, confused.

Summer's face shone with tears.

"My father, he did not know where the pelts went," Summer explained, holding back from breaking down into tears. "They were ours to sell. He worked hard, trapping the animals."

"Then why were they on our property if they were your pelts?" Gertrude responded bitterly. She turned to Mary, William, and Ed again before Summer could speak.

"My Hans, he found a heap, a big heap," she described, gesturing with her hands, "of thirty pelts one morning when he was working. Nice bunch, just lying there. And we need the money, you know that, Mary. So he took them into town and sold them. He found them!" she said passionately, trying to make everyone understand by talking more loudly.

"Found them where?" asked William.

"The police told me not to say yet," Gertrude replied mysteriously. "I'm not supposed to talk about details right now." She only paused briefly.

"But then her father," Gertrude said accusingly, pointing to Summer again, "he saw my Hans selling pelts and then he went crazy." The widowed woman twirled her index finger near her temple to make her point. "Her father screams 'Hey! These are my pelts!' and my Hans, he said 'Prove it!' But her father did not prove it. He did not prove anything! My Hans, he told him how he found them, on our property, just for us, we guessed. But her father, he went away angry, like this," she continued, baring her teeth in such a way that everyone was at least somewhat frightened by her vigorous storytelling.

Gertrude turned away and looked toward the fresh grave. A warm prairie wind raced across the fields and blew across the mound, stealing a thin layer of the soil. More tears formed in Gertrude's eyes as she spoke.

"The government, they promised that all of this land was free when we came here from Germany. You know what I think? I think nothing is free in this big place. I have all of this land. But I have nothing."

John felt sorry for Mrs. Schneider, but he could not believe River's Voice had committed murder. As the prairie sun climbed higher in the sky, he resolved in his mind to do something. John needed to find out the truth—wherever it might lead.

Chapter 5

Run-In at Borden

The fields of swaying golden wheat waved silently as the Diefenbaker Schooner rambled the seven miles towards Borden, while Summer rode her horse alongside the wagon. John was glad that it wasn't harvest time quite yet or there would be no time to think about anything else. Once harvest comes, getting the wheat threshed and to market is all that matters to anyone who farms. It takes many weeks of hard, intensive effort with every single family member contributing from sunrise to sundown. It's always an exciting time, but they were full days that left no extra minutes for anything else.

"Father," inquired Elmer, interrupting John's thoughts, "what did Mrs. Schneider mean when she said she had all that land but didn't have anything at all?"

"What do you think she meant, Elmer?" asked William, turning the question back on his youngest boy like any good teacher would.

"Well, did she mean she was all alone now?" Elmer asked.

William nodded. "That's certainly a big part of it, Elmer. The government gives you one hundred and sixty acres and they call it 'free.' But free is a mighty strange word when it takes every ounce of strength and determination one has just to make it work, especially in the beginning. Gertrude doesn't have any support now, so it's going to be even more difficult for her to get by."

Elmer nodded. Just then his father pointed off to the right, where a tiny, sod shack was collapsing under its own weight.

"There's another one of those free farms, son. Doesn't look like the people were able to do much with that gift, does it?"

Elmer and John's eyes traced over the sod shack, built with layers of grass and roots cut into strips. These were often temporary homes for settlers before they built something stronger. One side of the north wall had fallen in and prairie dogs scampered around it, rodent masters of the abandoned home. It was another homesteading failure, cause unknown. Cruel, hot summers were difficult enough and the winters that followed were colder than the imagination could stir up. There was unspeakable loneliness, disease, hunger. John knew his father was silently saying "Be thankful. We're doing alright." The prairies were certainly not for everyone. They were a gamble, a great roll of the dice by Canadian leaders to carve something—anything—out of a great unknown.

John squinted at Borden's familiar buildings, just now coming into view. The small but lively village was always a welcome break from the sameness of the homestead. Yet today, he didn't have the same excited feelings as the wagon carried William, John, and Elmer into town. Instead, he was anxious, wondering how to uncover the truth of a murder that the police had already determined was solved.

John's mother and uncle had been dropped off at the homestead after the funeral. He knew that he and Elmer would have double the usual work when they got back but it was worth it just to be able to go to town and do something different. The routines were very boring. It was a treat to take advantage of the opportunities to do something different as they came along.

If they didn't find Summer's grandparents in Borden, William had told Summer he would take her directly back home to her Long River reservation. Summer's horse, Prairie Dancer, walked calmly alongside Skipper and Blue, who were doing wagon duty. The majestic Pinto, with its paint design of distinctive brown and white patches, easily stood out from the two chestnut brown broncos. The horses got along well together, given how often Summer had visited in the past.

"Are you sure your grandparents are in Borden?" yelled William over the wagon noise to Summer.

"I think so, yes. Or maybe there are others from the village, since my grandparents do not feel well. Someone must be there to help my father," answered Summer intently. "Thank you for letting me ride with your family, Mr. D.," she added.

William grinned at Summer. When they had first met, he had given her permission to call him 'Mr. D.,' since Summer had a great deal of difficulty pronouncing the family's last name. While she had no problem with the pronunciation now, it was a term of affection that had stuck.

Summer, far more quiet than usual, watched the clouds flit across the sky. John tried to imagine what it must feel like to see your own father taken away by the police. He wasn't sure how he could help Summer but perhaps they would get some answers from the police.

As they entered Borden, William called out "Hello!" and tipped his well-worn hat to people that they passed. With few exceptions, he was cheerful and friendly, whatever was going on. William pulled the wagon off the road so that it was in front of the livery stable, where horses and wagons could be rented. The folks of Borden were proud of the livery stable because having one meant that the town was important and busy enough to keep such an establishment in business. Sometimes in the winter, when the local farmers went into town for the after-noon, they would park their horses at the stable to keep them warm and have them fed and groomed.

As he looked around, John could feel the village alive with activity. Women chatted near storefronts. Children stirred up clouds of dust as they chased each other in between buildings, their laughter hanging in the humid air. What John couldn't miss was the pungent smell of horse droppings scattered in foul piles all over the street.

The Diefenbakers and Summer parked several small buildings away from the Royal North West Mounted Police office, which also served as the local jail. John knew his father was trying to avoid drawing attention to themselves and didn't want anyone to guess that he was going to the police station. There were other horses nearby, all tied to posts, as well as a few more wagons parked along the street.

William hopped off the wagon and looked around. "Do you see your grandparents' wagon?" he asked Summer, who was tying Prairie Dancer to a tethering post.

She looked around and shook her head, perplexed.

William considered what to do next. "You three wait around here. Look around if you want but don't go far. I'm going to talk with the sergeant and find out what's going on."

"Mr. D., I want to come! I want to see my father," she pleaded.

William's eyes conveyed understanding, but he was firm in his statement. He lowered his voice as he approached and glanced around. "I don't want you in the jailhouse, Summer. It's no place for a young lady. I won't be long."

Summer nodded reluctantly and looked anxious as William walked away.

John felt sad for her. "Maybe Father will find out that your grandparents already got him released. Maybe he's back home right now."

But even John didn't sound convinced of this possibility, and it did nothing to brighten Summer's mood.

Elmer was deep in thought about visiting the jail, wondering what a real one looked like up close. As he shuffled around on the dirt road, he saw a small stone and kicked it, aiming for the open space of the middle of the street. Instead, the stone veered left, mistakenly striking a wooden post not more than a few inches from a tethered horse. Startled, the large brown horse took several steps back until it reached the end of its rope. The owner of the horse was just coming out of the livery stable and cast his gaze toward Elmer.

"Sorry, sir!" offered Elmer. "I didn't mean to do that."

"Indeed," the young man replied as he approached calmly, his dark facial hair obviously recently thinned at Svenson's barber shop. "You know, if my uncle were alive today, he would say children as old as the three of you should be put to better use, rather than wasting your days about the town."

John wanted to assure him that wasn't the case. "We're not wasting our days, sir. We're here because our father needed to come to town." John fixed his intense, dark eyes on the stranger.

Everyone agreed that John's eyes were his most noticeable feature because of their intensity. As he looked into the eyes of the stranger, John thought the same thing could be said of the man dressed in black. The man had a magnetic presence.

"I see," replied the man, pleasantly. He was tall, perhaps in his mid-twenties, and he stared at all three of them with an amused look. His dark clothes drew the warm summer sun. Although he was a stranger, John felt comfortable because of his easy nature.

"And where is your father?" he asked, glancing around. John paused. "Father is at the printing shop, buying a copy of the *Langham Times*," he responded hastily, hoping his fib was the right thing to do. He knew that his father didn't want any embarrassment to come to the family by being connected to the police station.

The stranger looked more closely at Summer, taking in her deerskin jacket, braided hair and facial features. His eyes brightened.

"Did you know that my uncle was fluent in Cree?" he asked, obviously recognizing her as Plains Cree.

"He knew the Cree language?" she asked, impressed.

The man laughed and nodded. "My dear, my uncle made it his business to know all of the Indian languages on the prairies, including French. He was Métis, you see. We were very close."

Métis, thought John. He would not have guessed the man in front of them was Métis. He wasn't dressed in the typical Métis fashion, which was a blend of European and Indian heritage clothing. Often they combined animal hides, like deer or elk, with flamboyant, colourful cloths. But nothing was certain any more—times were changing, John realized. This man was dressed plainly, in European-style clothing. In this case, he was dressed in black from head to toe.

"Who was your uncle?" asked Summer.

"My uncle," claimed the stranger with flourish "was Gabriel Dumont."

John hit Elmer in the arm to get his attention and his eyes widened. They had just met the person Sergeant English had been talking about!

"My name is André Dumont. It is a pleasure to meet you," he stated, now extending his hand. The children stood gaping-mouthed and shook his offered hand.

"And just who might the three of you be?"

"I'm John Diefenbaker, this is my brother, Elmer, and our friend, Summer Storm," John replied, wondering if he should have identified everyone to Mr. Dumont.

"I met Mr. Dumont, your uncle, a few years ago," John continued, "when we lived in Carlton. I was sorry to hear that he died a couple of years ago."

André blinked down at them and seemed to consider something for a moment. "Thank you, thank you indeed. He was a great man."

"Your last name is odd. German, I guess. Tell me," André

directed at John, the obvious leader of the youngsters. "Has anyone ever made fun of it?"

John looked to the ground briefly and nodded. "Yes, at school."

André nodded. "The treatment of folks not from Great Britain in this country is a terrible thing. The only thing worse is the treatment of the people who were here first. And Laurier does so little," he told them, referring to the Canadian prime minister, Sir Wilfrid Laurier. "Who will help change the attitudes of the people if not the leadership of the country?"

John wasn't sure if he was supposed to answer.

"Perhaps, people like us," André uttered, answering his own question.

"But hasn't Prime Minister Laurier opened the West to plenty of immigrants? There're folks from all over the world here," John pointed out.

"Bringing people is one thing," began André. "But you know that all these people are disturbing the lives of those who were here first."

John agreed with what André was saying. Through his studies with his father and uncle, and being friends with Summer, he had learned a lot about the changes endured by the Cree, other Indian tribes and the Métis on their way of life.

André seemed to read his mind and looked at Summer.

"It is dreadful the way the Cree and Métis have been pushed

around so much by the government. I know you are too young but your elders must miss the old ways."

Summer looked downcast. "Yes, they talk about it a lot."

An older Indian man walked slowly by and André glanced his way briefly and then continued more loudly.

"Everything has been mismanaged by the government. The Indians and Métis remember when the buffalo ran freely across the prairie, so thick that the herds were like great moving walls," he described, gesturing boldly. "What a proud time in our history, to remember the freedom we once had to do what was needed for our families and for our villages."

The man who had been walking by stopped a few feet away and listened attentively.

André continued. "I remember my uncle, Gabriel Dumont, who was so troubled at the treatment of the Métis and Indian peoples. The way the government land surveyors marched in, carving up the land in quarter sections, ignoring the preference for narrow fields that could touch the mighty waters of the North Saskatchewan River."

Just then a white couple walked out of the land titles office nearby and André noticed them, too. He seemed to quickly take in their possible concerns, too.

"And even the white settler has been lied to by the government. 'The Last Best West' the government calls it, and yet homesteaders often starve before they can yield a decent crop."

The white couple nodded at each other in agreement.

Seeing this, André continued. "And my people, the Métis, just like the Cree and other Indian tribes, are pushed farther and farther back to the sidelines to make way for progress. Well, I tell you I am tired of progress and tired of a government in Ottawa that is far away from what we experience here in the West."

"Here, here!" shouted someone.

John, Elmer, and Summer looked at one another, noticing how his words had quickly affected the other adults. He seemed to be able to get agreement from all kinds of people. Two men walked out of the blacksmith's shop a few businesses down the main street and began to walk toward André, while another couple emerged from the general store. The gathering seemed to happen spontaneously. As others began to approach, John felt it was time for the three of them to make an exit.

He bumped Elmer and caught Summer's eye, then the three slipped away through the adults and made their way in the direction of the police station, still listening to André Dumont's melodious voice, which carried easily through the air. He didn't seem to notice they had left, now that more adults had joined in.

"…and who will take up this challenge if not us? Who will protect our right to hunt where we need to hunt, to build where we need to build? Who will demand more railways be built…?"

With André's speech-making behind them, the three cut through between the blacksmith's shop and the livery stable, and walked along a back pathway behind the main stores. In between two unfamiliar buildings, they leaned against one of them to collect their thoughts.

"Now we know what Sergeant English and Mr. Wright were talking about. This André Dumont sure is trying to stir things up," John voiced.

"But why would he want to do that?" asked Elmer.

John shook his head. "Maybe he just wants to be famous, too. Like his uncle."

Looking around, John realized they were not in sight of the police station. "We should walk a bit closer to the station. Otherwise we'll miss Father when he comes out."

They walked along the dry ground, the faint noises of the main street nearby. As they passed between the side walls of two run-down businesses, they noticed a strong smell that made them turn their noses up. Just then, a man swore and there was a loud bang, as if a heavy object had fallen. This was followed by a conversation between two men that was getting louder and angrier. The three youths tucked themselves beside a building to take a look at the commotion without being noticed. John put his index finger to his lips.

"You overcharged me and you know it!" yelled one voice. "I want my money back, you thieving…"

Unfortunately, Elmer, who had been leaning over John and Summer, trying to hear better, fell over and rolled to the ground in full view of two men. As John and Summer scrambled to pull him back out of visual range, the face of one of the angry pair—a short, stocky man—flipped from anger to fear as he realized someone was watching. He averted his eyes quickly from John, Elmer, and Summer and stomped off angrily, muttering, "Forget it...just forget it."

The other man was quite large and boasted a scruffy, dirty beard. He wore a dark brown bent cowboy hat that looked like it had seen better days. There was a wagon behind him in the shadow of a building, filled with barrels and a canvas tarp pulled over more than half of them. He saw John look at the wagon and quickly pulled the tarp over the remainder of the barrels. Limping strongly and staring menacingly, the man took a few steps toward the three. John noticed a gun on his hip and pushed the others back a step.

"Now hold on, old Cecil's not going to hurt you," promised the grizzled man, clenching his soiled hands.

He grinned, yet his slate grey eyes were as hard as steel as he spoke.

"I think you three might have made a mistake in coming this way."

Chapter 6

Guilty Until Proven Innocent

John, Elmer, and Summer backed up rapidly as Cecil advanced.

For an overweight man with a limp, he moved surprisingly quickly, covering a great distance in a few hurried steps. His deeply-lined face was difficult to read.

"What's wrong with you kids? Don't you know where you're at?"

"We just want to walk by you, Mister," said John plainly, trying not to act alarmed.

"I'm afraid I can't let that happen," he replied, stopping in front of them and looking John in the eye.

John swallowed hard and Elmer and Summer began to retreat slightly behind him.

Just then a familiar, confident-sounding male voice interrupted.

"You can let them pass. Or you can deal with me."

André Dumont walked calmly from behind a nearby building, his eyes fixed squarely on Cecil. He moved a portion of his black vest aside to reveal his own gun holster, a quiet hint that he meant business.

Cecil's eyes narrowed. "This isn't any of your business, stranger."

They looked at each other oddly. "On the other hand, I believe I am quite certain about what your business is. Peddling illegal whisky from America out of the back of your wagon. So, the fact that you are even talking with three children disgusts me. Now move aside," said André sternly.

Cecil acted startled. "I don't know what you're talking about," he said indignantly. "I sell water."

Dumont laughed with skepticism. "The day the world chooses to buy water will surely be the end of civilization as we know it."

Cecil gestured behind him. "I was only trying to stop these kids from walking near this hotel. Drinking establishments are no place for children. Some mighty rough characters hang out around here."

"On that we can agree," said André. "And you appear to be one of them. But I don't think they are in any danger, as long as they hurry about their business and move quickly. You will move quickly, won't you?" asked André, looking at John, Elmer, and Summer.

"Yes sir," said John, who didn't need any further hints and began to quickly walk past Cecil, followed closely by Summer with Elmer at her heels.

"Don't forget what we talked about, young John!" called out André behind them. "This country needs real leadership!"

John nodded, although right now he was more concerned about weaving between the shadows of the two hotels to get back onto the main street of Borden.

John glanced back and saw André and Cecil still staring at each other, but he wasn't about to wait around to see how it ended.

As the three made their way up the sun-lit main street, they each gave a loud sigh of relief.

"Whew! That was too close," said Elmer, his eyes as large as supper plates. "Do you think that man was going to shoot us, John?"

"I don't think so, Elmer. But I'm glad we didn't have to find out."

"Thanks to André Dumont," said Elmer.

"Yes, I suppose so," said John, who was surprised by the gesture of help from the Métis man.

Summer suddenly pointed. "Look, your father!"

William had just exited the police station and was walking down the street toward the wagon, craning his neck, looking from side to side. He was obviously trying to see where his boys and Summer were.

"Father, over here!" said John waving and walking toward

him from an angle William obviously didn't expect. He wasn't about to tell him about the run-in with the stranger, Cecil, because it might spoil the freedom they currently had in Borden.

William looked curious. "Now just where were you three?"

"We were just looking around," Elmer answered, hoping the panic he felt moments before didn't show through in his voice.

John decided at the very least they should tell their father about observing André Dumont talking to others, and how a crowd had gathered around him while he spoke about the troubles of the Métis, the Cree, other Indian tribes and even settlers.

When he was finished, his father was looking around.

"Do you still see him?" asked William.

John, Elmer, and Summer looked around and shook their heads.

"This Mr. Dumont character sounds like trouble to me," said William. "Hopefully he won't be in town for very long."

"Did you see my father?" asked Summer eagerly, changing the topic.

William drew in a deep breath. "Yes, I saw him briefly but I spent most of the time talking with Constable Wood. He's the only officer there right now."

"Did Constable Wood say what happened?" asked John.

William looked downcast as he proceeded to tell Summer and the boys the facts of the case, as he understood them. The officer had spent a few minutes with William in a back room to be out of earshot of River's Voice's cell. As it turns out, William told Summer, after doing a thorough search of the Schneider property, they had found a necklace that looked like it might be Indian-made because it was a leather string with a series of shells. It was soon proven to belong to River's Voice.

As Summer tried to absorb this damaging information against her father, William had the unfortunate job of letting her know an even greater reason for her father being charged with the crime. Apparently there were also witnesses in Borden who said they heard River's Voice confront and threaten Hans Schneider about the pelts he was selling.

Summer began to shed tears, realizing the police seemed to have decided once and for all. She went and sat down on a nearby store step and Elmer went to sit beside her.

"Father," asked John, "what did the witnesses say they saw and heard?"

William sighed. "They say they saw River's Voice and Hans trying to pull the pelts from each other's hands. When Hans started to yell and attract attention, River's Voice apparently told Hans threateningly, 'You'll pay for this,' and then fled."

William turned to Summer. "I'm sorry, Summer. I wish there was more that I could do right now. If your father is innocent— and I believe he is—the truth will find a way to get out."

John was disappointed at the way his own father was being so optimistic and trusting that the situation would work itself out. He always talked liked that, John thought bitterly, even when things didn't work out. John needed an action plan. He wanted to gather facts and think this puzzle through. The odds were against justice for River's Voice. He was a Cree man and discrimination against Indians was all too common. John believed he couldn't just sit around and hope for the best.

However, Summer seemed to appreciate his father's words, John noticed.

"Do you know how my father got his name?" she asked. "How I got my name?"

The others shook their heads.

"My father, when he was just a baby, he hardly ever cried. And when he did make sounds, it seemed like they were sounds from music or nature. Everyone knew he would be a wonderful singer someday, so they called him River's Voice in the naming ceremony. But he never chose to sing as he grew up. His heart was always closed to singing. He did not use his gift.

"Then after my mother died of smallpox, when I was just six months old, he quietly started to sing to me. He was so sad. It was the middle of summer and our door was open. His voice grew louder and then all the others heard, too. The elders tell me his voice was so beautiful that everyone in the village stood to listen outside our house. Even though it had been many years since he sang, they said it was just like the river, the sweet sound it makes when it goes around rocks and fallen trees.

"One day, it started to rain but no one wanted to leave, even when storm clouds came. They would not leave the singing! When the four elders met for my naming ceremony, they knew my father's voice brought the mighty thunder. That's why they chose to call me Summer Storm.

"My father told the elders he would never forget his gifts again. He said his gifts were his wife, who cannot return, his daughter and his voice. Can he sing in prison, Mr. D.?"

John and Elmer remained silent after Summer's story, and William turned his head away for a moment. When he faced her again his eyes were damp.

"I think your father meant what he said. I think he will always find a way to sing," said William gently.

John let his mind drift to the beauty of the Cree naming ceremony. He pictured the rain falling on members of the village as they gathered around the home of River's Voice. It was strange to John how something sad and tragic could exist right beside something so beautiful.

"Your father confirmed for me that your grandparents are not feeling well right now," said William, changing subjects. "So with all the pressure on them and your extended family on the reservation, I offered your father to let you stay with us for a week. You're practically family anyway, as far as we're concerned. Of course, you'd have to help out with chores, too."

"I love your chores," said Summer jumping into the air and

smiling. She was thinking of the animals. "I would love to do this, thank you, Mr. D."

John and Elmer laughed.

William grinned. He was glad this news had cheered her up some.

"Elmer can sleep at Uncle Ed's, with John. You can have Elmer's spot, in the kitchen.

Summer nodded, happy that the Diefenbakers had room for her.

"I have to go to the land titles office for a little while and there's no room in there for everyone. We'll meet up at the general store in about twenty minutes to get Mother's supplies."

And with that, William left for the land titles office, while John took a good long look at the police station, not 50 feet away from them, once his father was out of sight.

"Let's go," he said, with Elmer and Summer in tow.

"Where?" asked Elmer.

"To the police station. I want to see Summer's father," answered John.

Elmer scrunched his forehead. "Father said we weren't allowed to go to the jail."

"No, he didn't. He said he didn't want Summer in the jailhouse because it wasn't a place for young ladies. He didn't say anything about us and I've got some questions for River's Voice."

Elmer considered John's technicality and looked impressed. "But I don't think Constable Wood will let us in, either," said Elmer.

"Actually, not us. Just me. But I need you, Elmer, to make this possible."

***

Constable Wood surveyed the cramped police office that he was now in charge of for three whole days. His boss, Sergeant English, was in Regina on official police business. He straightened some papers and looked around the room. To his right, he glanced up at his diploma from the Regina Police Academy. It inspired him to sit more smartly in his chair.

Almost reluctantly, he took a glance at his only prisoner in the corner, River's Voice, who solemnly returned his stare before speaking quietly and politely in his heavy, Cree accent.

"Constable, my people have always had respect for the Royal North West Mounted Police. Ever since the red coats showed up on the prairies, we knew they came to bring rules and order. I was only a young boy then. But now, what should we think? This is a mistake."

Constable Wood's face didn't change, but inside he felt unsettled. Why was he was feeling this way? Yes, his prisoner seemed to be a calm and polite sort of person. Yet, they had more evidence than they needed to lay a charge of murder against River's Voice. There was a bracelet found at the scene that he admitted belonged to him and even witnesses who say they heard him make threatening remarks when he argued with Hans Schneider. The man had a motive for the crime, Constable Wood told himself again. It doesn't matter what William Diefenbaker says.

"Just keep quiet in there," the constable said evenly. "You'll get a trial in Regina soon enough."

"Yes, you told me. A trial," repeated River's Voice calmly. "I think that really means I will never get to see my family again. I think that's what a trial means for me."

Constable Wood ignored the comment and returned to his paperwork. He was in charge now and he wasn't about to get distracted by anything. Just then he thought he heard the distant sound of his name.

"Officer Wood!" a young voice called.

Yes, he was sure he heard it that time.

"Officer Wood!"

Constable Wood slid his chair across the floor as he moved to open the door. He looked outside to his right and could see a young boy sitting on the ground, holding his ankle. Was that the youngest Diefenbaker boy?

"What's wrong there, young lad?" Constable Wood called back from the doorway.

Elmer grimaced. "I twisted my ankle! It really hurts! Can you help me?"

The constable hesitated, realizing he was the only officer in the station. Nonetheless, he got up from his chair, exited the station and pulled the door shut behind him. He walked over to where Elmer was on the ground, rubbing his ankle. When he had almost reached Elmer, John appeared from the side of the station where he had been peeking out and quietly began to enter the same door. He gave one last glance around to ensure no one would see him enter. Summer stayed in hiding. Her involvement would look more suspicious, since her father was in the jail cell.

John's eyes quickly found River's Voice in the lone cell to his right. John recognized the trademark tattoos on his arms and could see some of the tattoos on his chest, common for Plains Cree men. Things were changing for the Plains Cree, and for many other tribes, too. More and more white people were moving onto Native land and bringing their European customs. Indians still followed their ways of life but they were also trying to adopt white traditions. River's Voice's clothing was such an example. His shirt was made from moose hide but he wore light grey linen pants, a combination of the two cultures.

The man was surprised to see John enter.

"John! What are you doing here?" asked River's Voice, immediately standing and walking toward him in his cell. He extended his hand and John shook it and smiled.

"I don't have much time," John said quickly. "But I wanted you to know I don't believe you did…well, you know. I don't believe you killed anyone," said John, finding his confidence.

River's Voice tried to smile to show John his appreciation.

"Thank you, John. I know the Diefenbakers are good friends to my family."

"I want to help," John said calmly, "but I need to know something."

River's Voice nodded.

"Was that really your necklace on Mr. Schneider's property?" John asked.

The man nodded. "Yes, but I am not sure when I lost it. It could be the last time I visited that farm," said River's Voice. "It has round mussel shells on a leather band. But it was always loose at the part that joins," he said, gesturing with his two hands to help John understand.

John tried to figure out what he needed to know in the limited amount of time that he had.

"Did you have an argument with Mr. Schneider the day you were there?" John asked, glancing at the door and wondering how much time he had before Constable Wood returned.

River's Voice nodded. "Yes, I should not have gone again. That was a mistake. I tried earlier in the summer, too. He was very angry only because I am Indian. He didn't want me on his land, even though I tried to make a fair trade, like I do with your father," he explained. "He told me Indians were not welcome near farms and then I tried to talk some more, to try and find out why he was so mad at all Indians, but he just got louder and louder," River's Voice said. "So I left. And later that week, I realized my pelts were gone. They take so long to trap," he said, wistfully.

"How did you know Mr. Schneider had your pelts? And how did you come to know he was in Borden the day you saw him there?" asked John.

"A stranger left a message with one of the village elders who was sitting at the edge of our reservation. He said he heard Hans Schneider had something I wanted and that he was going to take it into Borden to get money. So I went there and watched for him and then I saw him in Borden with all my pelts! He took my pelts!"

John absorbed this information and was ready with another question. He was very good at remembering details.

"But didn't you tell the police this? Couldn't the village elder identify the man?"

River's Voice shook his head. "No, old Silver Fox is almost blind. He does not know what the person looked like."

"Where were you the night Mr. Schneider was killed?" asked John.

"Checking my traps in the woods. I had no money for food. I

had to work fast," the jailed man replied.

"By yourself?"

"That's what the police asked," said River's Voice, dejected. "Yes, just me. I have no way to prove this. What do you call that, John?"

"An alibi."

"Yes, I have no alibi." The Cree man looked discouraged.

John ran over to the window and looked outside. Elmer was talking up a storm with Constable Wood but it looked like the officer was getting impatient with him. It couldn't last much longer. He decided to switch topics.

"Summer really misses you but my father told her a jail is no place for girls, so she couldn't come inside," said John.

River's Voice took a deep breath and his eyes were misted over. "Your father is right. This is no place for her. Tell her I miss her. Tell her I have not stopped singing."

John nodded his head and smiled, happy that River's Voice understood.

"We'll do everything we can to figure out what really happened that night. We won't leave any stone unturned," said John.

River's Voice looked puzzled. "Stone…unturned?"

"Oh, it's an old saying," explained John, forgetting River's Voice wasn't likely to know common English sayings, given that he spoke Cree most of the time. "It means we will be very complete and thorough," said John.

He nodded appreciatively. "John, I don't know if anyone has enough time to help."

"What do you mean?" asked John.

"In six days I will be taken away from here to a larger prison in Regina. The trial will happen soon after."

"Regina! That's two hundred miles away! In that case," said John, "the way I see it is that we only have five days to figure this out."

Chapter 7

The Eagle and the Storm

For as long as John could remember, Taggart's General Store in Borden had always looked the same, at least from the outside. Its dark green roof and long, worn, wooden porch were as familiar as the back of his own hand.

Upon entering, though, it was hard to know what might be found. Sure, the necessities and old standbys were there—flour, salt, tea, animal feeds, and farm tools. Sugar and raisins and mixed nuts were scooped from large bins and weighed in brown paper bags. A great round of delicious-smelling cheese stood under a glass counter, which often competed with the aroma of freshly-ground coffee. It was a meeting place, too, where men talked about the weather and women converged on the dry goods side of the store, chatting about their children, neighbours or church get-togethers.

Each month, it seemed something new was added to the store: candy-striped treats on the counter, new clothing from Montreal or New York City, the latest marbles and balls and new dolls. All of it was shipped by wagon or train and it was exciting when new goods came in and were set up for sale.

Four or five times a year, for a couple of weeks each time, store owner Max Taggart left Borden, leaving his mother to run things. Some folks said he had a lady friend in Toronto. Others said he just liked to travel.

Actually, Max was a lot like his store. He always looked the same on the outside, but inside, you never knew what to expect.

He had a personality that was difficult to predict from one day to the next. To many, it was a surprise that he had gone into sales, since he didn't like to see people every day. He could be silent and unhelpful one day but rather pleasant the next.

"So how did you keep Constable Wood talking so long, Elmer?" John asked quietly as they walked up the steps of Taggart's General Store.

Elmer grinned.

"It wasn't too difficult, actually. At first I was just hollering about my ankle and how sore it was. But then I asked him if he thought a wrecked ankle would prevent me from joining the police academy in Regina. He seemed really impressed that I was thinking about being a police officer and he just started talking about his experiences. So I kept asking him more and more questions and then I saw you sneak out. I think I could have lasted another five minutes or so."

John slapped his brother on the back.

"Way to go, Elmer. I knew you could do it."

Elmer beamed as they met up with their father who had just exited the land titles office. They entered the store, just as a stranger passed them on his way out. Elmer darted over to the marble bags that hung like bulging treasure from small metal hooks. Summer immediately drifted over to the candy jars up on the counter, while John tried to restrain himself from moving anywhere too fast. He felt he might be getting too old to immediately run toward toys or candy. However, his brother's frantic calls for him to come at once to see the new marbles soon wore away John's resolve.

"William! Good to see you!" said the Max Taggart that liked people. After also waving to John and Elmer and glancing at Summer, John tried to listen in to what William and Max were talking about.

John realized Max was obviously curious about Summer, wondering what she was doing with the Diefenbakers. William explained what had happened, although the store owner had certainly heard about the murder of Hans Schneider, just like everyone else in town.

Max's voice was very low at first, and John couldn't hear every word.

"Are you sure? Innocent?" he asked skeptically.

William nodded. "Of course. There has to…explanation," William replied quietly, too, obviously happy Summer was out of hearing range. It bothered John that most people assumed that River's Voice was guilty. He knew that it had something to do with the community mistrusting Indian people. Few people liked Hans Schneider. On the other hand, he was white, not Indian. This unfairness frustrated John.

Max raised his voice slightly now and John could hear the conversation better.

"…a tragedy, that's what it is. You know, I hate to talk out of school, so to speak, but I just wonder if Gertrude's going to be able to clear this debt off."

"Debt?" William asked obligingly.

Max nodded. "They weren't doing so well, financially. It's hard for everyone but they seemed to have an especially hard time, after that fire last year knocked off half their crop. Lucky you weren't swept up in that, too."

William nodded his head. "I remember."

Max pulled on the ends of his long dark moustache, which curled at the ends. "Yes, I felt sorry for them so I started to run a tab. I finally had to quit, though, because they just weren't making an effort to pay me back. Old Hans wasn't too happy with me, but you know what? I wasn't too happy with him either. I mean, times are tough for everyone, right? I tried to do them a favour but I'm not running a bank here."

"It was nice of you to try and help out," William said diplomatically.

This seemed to satisfy Max a great deal. He helped William find the various supplies he needed to take back to the homestead. Mary had given him a small list that included coffee, flour and a few canned goods, as well as grain for the chickens.

Although John, Elmer, and Summer lingered at the counter near the candy sticks, William was firm.

"Sorry you three, there's no money for that today," William said.

Max, feeling generous, reached over for the jar of red-striped candy sticks.

"If it's okay with you, William," he said looking his way "then it's on me today. How does that sound?"

Elmer and Summer looked with anticipation at William, who nodded and gave them a wink.

"Yes, thank you! Yes, please!" said the two of them with looks of delight on their faces.

Max held the jar in front of Elmer and then John but seemed to pause for the briefest of moments before holding it in front of Summer.

"Thanks, Max," said William, "that's generous of you."

"Not at all, not at all," he replied.

"Okay everyone, let's get going," William said, as they all said goodbye and walked down the wooden steps toward their wagon.

Max Taggart stood near the door and muttered quietly to

himself, pulling on his long moustache.

***

When the wagon and Summer, on her majestic Pinto, arrived at the Diefenbaker homestead, the sun had already fallen significantly from its high perch in the sky. The heat didn't waver in intensity, hanging in uncomfortable humidity. The sky was dark to the west but it still seemed to be a distant concern.

Ed Diefenbaker was busy working outside on the new well that had to be built. Mary Diefenbaker was chopping vegetables outside on a makeshift table in a shaded area, where she had escaped the confines of her tiny, dark kitchen.

Prairie Dancer dutifully walked alongside the wagon for the five mile trip from the Long River reservation where the Diefenbakers had travelled for Summer to pick up clothing and other things that she would need for her week-long stay. When she asked William if her *masinasowatim* could come—Cree, for Pinto—he thought about it and couldn't think of any reason to say no, as long as she took care of the mare herself. This was good news for John and Elmer, who delighted in the idea of horseback riding with Summer, at least during the times when Skipper and Blue weren't needed to pull the wagon.

If John and Elmer could be considered good riders, John thought to himself, Summer was even better. Summer had owned the horse since she was three years old. It didn't make a difference how hard times got, her father had promised her that they would never sell the horse. He had kept his word. Prairie Dancer was her pride and joy.

Summer jumped down from her mare with a grin on her face and waved to Mary and then to Ed, who was farther away. John realized that with all the trouble her father was in, staying with friends must be a welcome diversion for her.

Mary smiled and welcomed Summer, giving her a warm hug. John and Elmer quickly took over the task of unhitching Skipper and Blue from the wagon, something they had mastered long ago. John waved Summer over towards them so that the three of them could work on cooling down the horses. They grabbed some brushes and chatted excitedly while the adults unloaded the supplies.

Mary fussed over the goods that William had brought home and she soon let him know what mistakes he made shopping. Ed, who had since joined them, gave William a sympathetic look and then appeared amused as he reached down for the tail ends of his shirt and used them to wipe his sweaty face.

Mary didn't waste any time reminding the boys of their promises to catch up on their chores.

"You're lucky you've now got an extra pair of hands to help out," she called out, referring to Summer.

"I get Summer for my chores!" John called out.

"No way!" said Elmer. "I need her!"

"Summer can take turns helping you both out," said Mary sternly. "And don't talk about the girl like she's a farm tool, either!"

"Yes, Mother," the boys said, almost at the same time. John, Elmer, and Summer finished their brushing and then set the three horses out to pasture in the north field.

***

All the chores, other than cleaning out the animal paddocks, were done by seven o'clock. Mary told them to get cleaned up for supper and finish afterwards. Once everyone sat down, they joined hands and recited their prayer of grace. Everyone enjoyed Mary's meal—wild duck that Uncle Ed had shot early that morning, with potatoes and small carrots. For a special treat, in anticipation of Summer coming, Mary had also baked a Saskatoon berry pie, made with the large berries that had an apple-like flavour. Summer shared that the Cree name for the berry was *misaskwatomina*. It was one of her favourite fruits.

"Mother, thank you for this delicious dinner," John said, as he leaned over and gave her a one-armed hug. The others mumbled and nodded in agreement with their mouths stuffed with food. It seemed like everyone just wanted to avoid talking about Summer's father, if only for the first night.

Summer felt so welcome at the Diefenbaker table. She spoke about her life on the reservation, and how the adults struggled to make a good life for their children. Although Chief Five Hawks worked hard, nothing seemed to ever change. The Diefenbakers could relate to struggling to get by on the farm. They added how difficult it was to get a fair price for wheat after the harvest.

"The sky looks strange tonight and the air is so heavy and sticky," said William, glancing out at the eerie glow of the falling sun. "I think Mary's right. We're in for a storm."

Ed pushed his plate away as he finished and nodded in agreement at his brother's comment. "That's alright, we need the rain," he said. "Looks like we'll have a pretty good crop this year."

Everyone smiled at the thought of a good harvest and then the clean-up process began. After the table was cleared, Mary shooed her boys and Summer out of the house. It was time for the children to finish their daily chores. Summer enjoyed the evenings with John and Elmer, even though it meant cleaning out the animals' paddocks.

"What do we do tomorrow?" asked Summer, wiping a few stray hairs away from her eyes. She seemed to be enjoying everything, simply because it wasn't part of her normal routine.

"Probably the same thing," said Elmer miserably.

"Great!" said Summer while John and Elmer glanced at each

other and shook their heads.

The animals seemed restless—even the oxen and not much usually bothered them. John chalked it up to the lightning flickering far away.

***

After putting in a hard day's work, Ed fell promptly asleep that night. Although John and Elmer had worked hard, too, they lay on their backs with their eyes wide open, heads resting on the folded blankets they used for pillows. John was in his usual place, his single wooden bed shoved against the north wall of the tiny homestead. Elmer was right below him camped out on the floor. They both stared at the tiny window in front of them, watching the distant lightning play about the sky. As they stared at the ribbons of fractured light, Elmer sat up on one elbow and leaned over to John, sensing he was still wide awake, too.

"John?" he whispered.

"Yes?" John whispered back, leaning over on one elbow too.

"Do you think Summer will get to come back during the harvest?"

"I don't know," said John. "We could ask Father and Mother. She did last year, remember?"

Elmer nodded but it was too dark for John to see.

"John?"

"Yes?"

"Do you think all of us will get to go to Langham later this week when Mother sells her butter?"

"I hope so," said John, whispering.

"John, if they say River's Voice did you-know-what and he has to stay in jail for a long time, do you think Summer can always live with us?"

"He didn't do it," said John quickly.

"I know that," said Elmer. "I said what if they say he did?" he repeated.

"Probably not, Elmer. She still has family, you know."

As much as he loved the idea of Summer staying with them, John disliked the idea of someone getting blamed for something they didn't do.

"I don't want to think about that right now, Elmer," John complained. "I've got a better idea. Why don't you try to help me figure out who really did it and then we won't even need to have this conversation?"

"You mean, like, solving it...like the police do?" he clarified.

"Yes," said John. "Like the police."

Elmer gave this some thought. "Summer would want to help, too," he concluded.

Ed stirred and turned over in his bed, just as brilliant lightning briefly illuminated the walls in the small shack. For about two seconds, John and Elmer could see each other propped up in their beds and Elmer quickly made a scary face with his eyes wide like saucers. John reached out and thumped his brother on the shoulder.

"Oww!" said Elmer, slightly above a whisper.

"If you wake Uncle Ed, he'll make you sleep outside," said John. He delighted in the way he imagined his brother's face looking now. John wished more lightning would flash so he could see his expression. However, the storm must have been too far away because the homestead remained in darkness.

"Well, I'm tired anyway. Goodnight," said Elmer, barely whispering.

John grinned in the dark. "Good night, Elmer."

***

John returned to the scene of the murder in his dream. He was too late—again—and Hans Schneider lay dead, his head propped onto his wife Gertrude's lap. The same red blood began to spread across the man's clothes and John was terrified. Gertrude began to wail and John squeezed the sides of Skipper to prompt him to race home. As Skipper approached a fallen tree, the horse froze in fear, sending John flying through the air. John landed hard. He woke sweating in his bed and breathing heavily.

He closed his eyes and tried to let go of the anxiety from his dream. John thought of something peaceful as he tried to get back to sleep—a fishing trip he went on with his father. But where was his father?

The great bald eagle sat calmly on the banks of the mighty North Saskatchewan River. It didn't seem to realize that John was there, observing. Soon it was joined on the left by a buffalo that could walk on two legs who also observed the eagle's movements with contentment. On the eagle's right, many spotted horses galloped up to sit beside the eagle, their breath coming in gentle snorts.

The eagle was using its wings to scoop up the sand along the banks of the river and filter it between its feathers. John sensed that it was a hot day in the middle of summer. For as far as he could see, there was only blue sky punctured by groupings of trees to the north. As the eagle closed its eyes, a cool wind seemed to come from nowhere and ruffle its white head feathers.

Then, the eagle reached down and scooped water from the river in its cupped feathered wings. John began to understand the eagle was interacting with three of the four elements— earth, air, water.

But where was fire?

Just then the bald eagle arranged large stones in a circle, creating a fire pit. The bird brought out a pointed flint stone and struck down on a small rectangular-shaped piece of steel over some dry grass that he had placed inside the perimeter of stones, calmly lighting the fire in the traditional Indian way.

There it is, thought John as he observed. Fire.

As the eagle sat there for a moment and tended its small fire, some of the flames leapt over the protective circle of rocks to the dry land. The eagle was startled.

It grasped the stray flames with its feathered wings and suddenly turned to John, holding the fire, staring at him in his dream as if all along it had known that John was there. John felt frightened as the eagle held onto the flames with its cupped, feathered wings and began to walk toward him.

"No, get away," mumbled John, trying to shout. "It's fire… dangerous. Fire….It's fire!" he tried to scream at the top of his lungs, but it seemed as if he could hardly speak at all.

Chapter 8

Everything in its Path

"Get up! John! Get up!"

John opened his eyes to see his uncle and brother dressing quickly. They looked terrified, glancing nervously out the tiny shack's window. The small room was lit by a strange glow from the window, even though it was obviously still the middle of the night. Ed flung open the door and ran outside and as he did so, the room was bathed in a warm, orange light. He shouted over his shoulder to Elmer and John as he ran toward the main house.

"You boys come to the house. Let's go!"

"What's going on?" asked John, scared and confused as he dressed quickly.

"You're the one who was shouting 'fire' and woke us up!" exclaimed Elmer, stuffing his feet into his shoes. "The whole prairie is on fire, John!"

John stumbled over to the doorway, a fragment of his strange dream about an eagle beginning to come back into his mind. He then looked outside to see the darkness cut by a wide swath of brilliant orange fire in the distance, gorging on the dry grass that stood in its way. He felt his stomach knot in fear as he realized the sheer size of the great blaze. A grass fire—the thing homesteaders feared most.

John and Elmer raced across the dry ground, imagining their own homestead engulfed in flames. Ed's shack seemed to be further away and safe for the moment. And yet, it was possible that everything they owned—their home, their barns, their crop of wheat—would be lost under the torrent of fire racing across the land in the distance. As they ran, they watched the fire grow in intensity in the distance, a pulsing roar they could even smell as it gobbled up the countryside.

The thirsty land over the past couple of weeks had created the perfect conditions for the deadly lightening strikes overnight. John imagined that when they had gone to bed with lightning flashing in the distance, it must have struck a dry tree. The resulting strike would have splintered the tree, creating deadly sparks that would have fallen on the tinder-dry grasslands of the prairies. With nothing but wide open dry grasslands, the fire would have grown like a flash.

As they closed in on the main homestead, John and Elmer saw their father come running out with his shirt half on, almost colliding with Ed, who had been screaming his brother's name the whole way. The two of them now worked together, shouting to each other about what was best to do. William saw Elmer and John running toward the house. He yelled for them to stay close to the home, just as Mary and Summer quickly made their own exit.

Mary gathered John, Elmer, and Summer together and tersely issued instructions. "Get towels and rags and wet them from the two water barrels. Then line the bottoms of the doorways."

With anxious faces everyone did as they were told, knowing how precious water was but also understanding the threat.

John knew his father and uncle were about to do the only possible thing that might save them from the fire's path of destruction. They were going to hitch the horses to a plough and dig deep furrows in the land all around the property. Hopefully, when the fire reached the freshly dug black earth it would have no new dry grass to feast on and simply stop at that exact point where the grasses burned off.

The animals in their paddocks were restless, pacing around and smelling the burning air. William and Ed led Skipper and Blue out of the barn but the horses were afraid of the danger that they sensed. Both of them resisted and began to tug their massive heads backwards.

John stole glances at his father and uncle who were frantically trying to hitch up the horse team to the plough. He knew it made sense to use the horses, rather than the oxen, because horses could do the job more quickly and time meant everything now. John wished he was helping them, rather than wetting rags. He felt he could assemble the team faster than them if given the chance.

"Dang it! Whooaa!" William bellowed, trying to get control of Skipper while Ed tried to do the same with Blue.

"Father, let me help!" called out John.

William glanced over at John and nodded.

John raced toward the team but slowed down as he got nearer to avoid scaring them further. He talked reassuringly but firmly to Skipper and Blue. John could hear Summer's horse, Prairie Dancer, in the barn obviously feeling the stress of the events taking place.

"That's it…good boy…good boy. Easy now," soothed John. He then nodded to his father and uncle who were about to lean over and attach the pair of animals' gear to the plough.

John kept stroking the horses' necks and talking to them as he watched the spectacular fire rage in the distance, wondering how anything could be so beautiful to see and yet so destructive. John recalled his uncle telling him that prairie fires can move as fast as six hundred feet per minute and burn as hot as seven hundred degrees Fahrenheit. It was always supposed to be something to know, not experience.

While the thunder and the lightning were still cracking and illuminating the sky, there was no rain to depend on, although everyone was hoping the downpour would finally come. The dull rumble of thunder along the vast, open space was ominous.

With the team hitched up, Father began to plow as deeply into the dark earth as quickly as possible in order to save what little was theirs—the tiny house, barn, sheds and animals. As well, about forty loads of hay stood in a corner that would not last thirty seconds if fire touched it.

The horses responded like well-trained soldiers for William. Despite the threat of the wall of fire that marched steadily toward the homestead, they continued to haul their plough, turning over the rich soil in a wide furrow all around the haystack and buildings. Ed bolted over and yelled something to William, who nodded.

William then steered the horses over to a new area farther away from the buildings, skipping about fifty yards of ground from the ring he had just ploughed around the property. The team dug up a second parallel, wider ring of dirt around the homestead. By creating this other band of fresh soil, John realized they were hoping to create a buffer zone to stop the fire even further back. Elmer, Summer, and Mary looked up and watched as they continued with their own work.

After William finished ploughing the second ring and was safely inside the inner ring, Ed rushed over with a flaming torch he had lit and lowered it to set fire to the ring of grassland between the two ploughed circles. Some of the flame leapt back at him, catching him on his arm.

"Aghhh!" Ed yelled, clutching his bare skin.

"Uncle Ed!" John yelled, starting to go towards him until his mother pulled him back.

"You stay put, boy," said his mother, who was concerned but was not about to let John get hurt, too. Ed, having lit the ring of grass successfully, then jumped back into the inner ring with everyone else. Everyone backed up together.

Even though it was still dark—long before the rising sun— the skies were ablaze in jagged, orange light. The fire wall that had at one time seemed so distant now barreled towards the Diefenbakers' property with ferocious speed while the smaller fire roared to meet it. Ed's smaller ring of fire began to subside, leaving only the black, burnt grass stubble and charred ground.

The larger fire roared toward them, only seconds away, eating all dry grass in its path.

"Father!" hollered John. "We have to help Mrs. Schneider. We have to plough around her farm, too!"

"There's no time, John!" his father yelled back. "All we can do now is watch," he said in a lower voice, his heart heavy with anxiety as he prayed for his neighbour's safety.

William put his arm around Mary and the others stood close to one another in solidarity. When the fire reached the border of ploughed land before the Diefenbaker's land it raged against its captivity. But there was nothing left for it to burn in this area. It then whooshed around the perimeter of the homestead and began to race away to new destinations.

Everyone cheered and hugged each other, although Ed still favoured his burnt arm. Just as John expected, Mrs. Schneider's field was next. As the flames bore down on her farm, the Diefenbaker group watched helplessly and wondered how much would be destroyed. Within a few minutes the sky opened up, answering with a powerful rain that came down in torrents. It gushed down thick, wet droplets, as the storm born of desperate humidity was finally released. The Diefenbakers and Summer had never been so happy to be caught outside in the rain. Soon the pounding deluge would overcome the fire's appetite and ensure new fires wouldn't begin tonight. Nature had taken so much in the last few minutes. Now, in balance, it was set to give back to replenish the scarred earth.

**

It was a busy morning cleaning up and organizing the farm after the close brush with disaster the night before. Gertrude Schneider lost more than a third of her wheat, William estimated, before the rain had quelled the flames. It was another blow to the poor woman, John thought, so soon after the loss of her husband.

"Will the government help Mrs. Schneider? She'll need money to live on," John queried his father.

"That would be nice but I'm afraid there's no such thing," he explained.

John didn't think this was fair, given that it would be difficult for someone to carry on all alone. He was glad that his mother had gone over to Mrs. Schneider's to check on her. Mary was worried about her and wanted to let her know that neighbours cared about her. Even with this latest catastrophe, John couldn't help but feel frustrated. Mrs. Schneider could still not shake her belief that Summer's father killed her husband. The boy had to admit that with River's Voice arrested, why would she believe anything else? And now, there were only five days until River's Voice would be transferred to Regina and likely convicted, unless new evidence was found. John felt the weight of time bear down. He needed to prove his innocence in four days to save him from being sent to trial.

The humidity that had enveloped the prairie for weeks had finally broken during the big storm, leaving dry warmth in its place. After their work was done, John, Elmer, and Summer took the horses for a scouting ride to report back on the damage to the north, where the fire had begun. Although they loved to ride along the once-familiar trails, the blackened ground and absence of vegetation was sad to see. It was as if wide bands of land were eaten alive by the fire, with no mercy shown to anything in its path. There were some swaths of land that somehow remained unaffected, their higher slopes a curious stripe of patchy green, which the horses gratefully grazed on when they stopped for a break.

John turned his mind to the damaged wheat fields. He knew that his own family was fortunate, since their field was relatively unscathed, other than a small corner, thanks to his father and uncle's swift efforts. Ed's property was also saved since it was south of William's and the rain had extinguished the flames before they reached it.

As John surveyed the land in front of him, his nose was repulsed because the usually sweet smell of the long grasses was now an overpowering burnt stench. John squeezed his nostrils shut for a moment's break. He knew that fire could not completely destroy the prairie grasses because of their deep roots. But it would be some time before the lush green and golden hues in this area would return in fullness.

"Look," said Summer, pointing in the direction of the Diefenbaker land, about three quarters of a mile behind them. From where they were standing on a slope, John and Elmer swivelled around to observe the patches of golden wheat waving in between deeply-charred fields.

"We sure were lucky," said John quietly.

"Yes, lucky you woke us up, shouting 'FIRE,'" said Elmer. "But it was sure weird how tired you acted after that."

John described his dream for his brother and Summer. There were the horses and the buffalo and the great bald eagle that had warned him of some danger by moving toward him carrying an open flame in its wings. Summer seemed very interested.

"John, this may be your animal totem," she said simply.

"My animal totem? What do you mean?"

"The Cree believe everyone has at least one special animal to watch over them, to guide them when they are in trouble. Sometimes it takes many years to find. Sometimes there are more than one animal. Maybe yours is the eagle," she said, noting the prominent role the eagle played in his dream.

John had never thought about having an animal association. He liked the idea—and liked the eagle, with its strength and powerful vision. There were many bald eagles in the forests of northern Saskatchewan, but they were rarer near the wheat fields. He also liked buffalo, although in real life they were almost gone now after years of over-hunting. The spotted horses he dreamt about must symbolize that he had always liked horses.

"Do you have an animal, Summer?" John asked, curious.

"Yes. Right here," she said, smiling at Prairie Dancer.

"Of course!" said John. It only made sense for Summer.

"How come I don't have an animal?" asked Elmer, interrupting the flow.

"You do. You have Lily," teased John, naming the family's cow. Elmer shoved him good-naturedly.

Summer explained. "For me, I always loved horses and I

grew up with her," she said, stroking Prairie Dancer's long nose.

"She is a part of me. Even when I was only small, like this," she said, holding her hand off the ground until it was about the height of a two year old, "I wanted to be near the horses."

"They let you be near horses when you were that small?" Elmer asked in disbelief.

Summer's face lit up with the happy memories. "It was safe. The horse is my totem, remember? Everyone could tell. That's why my father got Prairie Dancer for me when I three. Getting her is my first memory," she said, patting the majestic horse's neck.

"I don't remember everything, but my father told me he said, 'Bless this horse and bless my daughter, Summer Storm, who will one day ride like the wind.'"

"You already do that," said Elmer. "That's for sure!"

A clattering sound made everyone turn at the same time. As the three peered down the length of rough trail, they could make out the distinct shape of a carriage and horses, wobbling its way toward them.

John stared. "Is that who I think it is?" he asked.

***

At the Schneider homestead, Mary brought the coffee cup to her lips and tried to read all of the emotions that played about

Gertrude Schneider's face. She had been through so much, beginning with losing her husband only three days ago. Now, a third of her crop was burned to the ground. If the Lord had a plan for this poor woman, thought Mary, she prayed it would soon be revealed.

"I want you to know that when the threshers come in a few weeks, we'll make sure your crop gets done. You're going to make it," said Mary soothingly.

Gertrude's eyes were dull but she nodded in appreciation.

"Thank you, Mary. Your family is always so kind," she replied with her heavy German accent. "But I don't care about the crop any more."

Mary tried to understand what she was hearing. "You'll need your crop, Gertrude. This is how you're going to survive. Everyone's going to pitch in and help, you'll see. I'll have lots of canned goods by then and I know…"

Gertrude began shaking her head even before Mary had finished speaking.

"I will not stay here," she said, looking around her small house. "I have a sister in Bavaria," she said quietly, almost without emotion. She slowly raised her own coffee to her lips and slurped loudly.

"Bavaria? You mean Germany?" asked Mary astonished. "Gertrude, you have all this land. Hans would have wanted you to stay and…"

"Hans!" shouted Gertrude, setting her coffee down too hard as hot liquid splashed out on the table and on her hand. Her eyes instantly brimmed with tears. "Hans is not here to tell me what to do. Hans is not here to see me go!" She rubbed the warm liquid from her hand, her eyes locked with Mary's.

Mary remained quiet.

"I'm too old, Mary. Too old and alone," Gertrude finished.

Mary stood up slowly and reached for a cloth hanging in Gertrude's kitchen area, calmly wiping up the spilled coffee. The older woman just stared out the small window at the promise of more sun. Then she spoke softly.

"I've already made arrangements to sell the farm. I have enough money to take a train from here, to get to a ship in Montreal. They will send me the farm money later. I don't care."

Mary wasn't sure if she dared to offer advice, but she was going to try.

"Gertrude, it's been such a short time. Are you sure you feel you've made the right decision?"

The widow nodded. "I made up my mind on the night he died. I will leave this place. Nothing will change that."

***

Earl T. Wright brought his brilliant canary yellow wagon to a halt in front of John, Elmer, and Summer and peered down at them, tipping his black hat and smiling.

"Well, hello there," he said in his trademark drawl. "It sure is good to see you after this mess," he said, glancing at the blackened fields. "How is everyone? How badly were you hit by the fire?"

"We were lucky, Mr. Wright. It barely touched us, thanks to Father and Uncle Ed plowing furrows in time. Except, Uncle Ed burnt his arm some and Mrs. Schneider lost more than a third of her crop," said John dejectedly.

"Well now, that's good news for your family as far as your crop goes. I'm sorry to hear about your uncle's arm. I should stop in and see if he needs a good old fashioned Rawleigh's Man remedy. But what a shame Gertrude was hit so hard. And so soon after her husband's death. Too many fine folks were hit hard from what I've seen."

Elmer had moved a bit closer to the wagon. "What's that, Mr. Wright?" he asked, pointing to a collection of items half covered by a sheet. Now all three looked at the space behind Earl and saw a collection of tools, a basket filled with something they couldn't see and a few books.

"Oh, that's nothing," said Earl, quickly covering it completely with the sheet. "Just some blankets I like to keep. I do so much travelling so they're nice to have. Sometimes I have to sleep in the carriage you know."

John, Elmer, and Summer just nodded but no one said anything. Earl cleared his throat.

"Well now, I best be off. You three take care, hear?"

And with that, the canary yellow wagon carrying the Rawleigh's Man departed down the uneven trail.

Chapter 9

Chief Five Hawks

Summer Storm was a born rider. It was hard to tell where she ended and Prairie Dancer began, John thought to himself, as she entertained the boys with trick riding during the five-mile ride to her reservation the next morning.

Although they were trying to have fun along the way to the Cree reservation, the truth of their mission was more serious. Ed's burn from the prairie fire seemed deeper than they first thought and Mary was worried her home plaster remedy was not working. Summer had volunteered to pick up an ointment her grandparents had on the reservation. It was something that had been passed down for generations by the Cree and Summer felt that it was a way she could make another contribution to the Diefenbakers for letting her stay.

As she resumed her trick riding, she lay on her back, sideways, while her Pinto kept on trotting. The boys laughed and trotted along more calmly beside them as she then stood on the horse's back, perfectly balanced, while Prairie Dancer stayed the course. Its lithe body was in tune with Summer's subtle movements. Only once, when the horse had to turn slightly to avoid a protruding bush in the otherwise flat field, did Summer falter, but as she fell she grabbed her horse's neck. The strong Pinto held fast while it ran until Summer pulled herself around, only this time not as gracefully. She was laughing so hard at her own mishap that the boys realized it was alright to join in.

John and Elmer had asked their parents for permission to go for the trip to the reservation, too. It would give them a chance to get out with Skipper, Blue, and Prairie Dancer for a good long ride. Yesterday's ride of only a few farms' distance was depressing, since the youths witnessed the fire damage to their neighbours' properties.

Today's ride was more enjoyable.

"We're getting close," said John, pointing into the distance.

John then turned his thoughts inward. Elmer knew his brother was thinking because he got very quiet and his forehead became furrowed. It was like he forgot he was with other people, even though Elmer and Summer were talking. Elmer was used to this although, as the younger brother, he felt like it was his solemn duty to try and find out what was going on inside his brother's head—usually before his brother was ready.

"John, what are you thinking about?" Elmer asked, after some minutes had passed.

John paused before he spoke. "Just what we were talking

about yesterday evening, you know, seeing Mr. Wright."

"Yes, that was strange," Elmer said, recalling his own memory. "What do you think all of that stuff was inside Mr. Wright's wagon?"

"Well, we saw a basket with something in it, some tools and some books. There was nothing that looked really suspicious," John answered.

"Then why did he hide those things?" asked Summer.

John nodded. "That's just it. Why would he lie about it just being blankets, when we clearly saw other things underneath? I still don't understand what he was concealing. What was he really worried about?"

The others fell silent, lost in their own thoughts of the strange encounter with Earl T. Wright. Prairie Dancer seemed to know she was closer to home, as she was making gentle noises while she walked. Skipper and Blue were just happy to be on an adventure, especially through an area that had been untouched by the destructive hand of the prairie fire.

"Aren't we close to the river?" John asked, referring to the mighty North Saskatchewan.

Summer nodded. "It's near here. There's a place where the river bends near the forest," she replied, pointing, "where I have been swimming before."

"Let's go swimming!" said Elmer enthusiastically. "I mean, after we get the ointment."

"Can we do that?" asked Summer, who seemed keen.

John instantly felt uneasy about the idea for a number of reasons. Father and Mother had told them before not to swim in the North Saskatchewan River because it had a strong current and the boys weren't very good swimmers. On the other hand, John reasoned, they were with Summer and he knew she was an experienced swimmer. John didn't want to feel like the one who was about to spoil all the fun.

"What about the current?" John asked, trying to maintain some sense of responsibility.

"It's fine where I swim," said Summer. "As long as you don't go far into the middle, you'll be alright," she said convincingly.

John considered for another minute. "Fine with me, but we won't be able to stay long."

"Yes!" whooped Elmer, happy that his older brother wasn't going to rain down on all the fun.

"Our clothes should dry on the way back easily enough, with all this sun," John continued. "But you know if we get caught we won't be able to go to Langham tomorrow to help sell Mother's butter."

Elmer had almost forgotten about the trip. "We won't stay long," he said reassuringly.

"But first let's get the ointment," John reminded them.

With the reservation now in view, John looked at the simple collection of small, plain wooden homes that had replaced the famed Cree tepees of old. John had once seen two tepees with his father when they were travelling for supplies, but it wasn't common anymore. Two hunters had set them up for a temporary camp and John was invited inside to see what they were like. It was an experience he never forgot.

Closer to their destination, John and Elmer fell back in formation to let Summer lead the way to her grandparents' house. People in the village who were working outside peered up with curiosity as the unlikely trio entered the village. Small children ran toward them, waving and laughing to Summer and the boys. She was delighted to see the little ones and spoke to them in both Cree and English, introducing John and Elmer who were still on horseback behind her. She called them *nitoótém*, which the boys learned meant 'my friend' in Cree. John responded by nodding and smiling, while Elmer waved enthusiastically. In fact, Elmer did it for so long that John was beginning to feel uncomfortable.

"Elmer, stop waving so much. It's embarrassing," said John in a low voice.

Elmer frowned at his older brother. "Who made you the chief? I'm just being friendly."

John groaned.

Along the way Summer pointed out various things on the reservation, like the building where she went to school and where Chief Five Hawks lived. John saw a magnificent looking sorrel-coloured bronco tied in front of Chief Five Hawk's place. It seemed familiar, but he couldn't place where he had seen it. When they neared Summer's house, John could see the expression on her face change, as she probably pictured her father inside, safe and free, instead of locked up in a jail cell.

Soon Summer slowed her horse and jumped off, a few feet away from her house where she lived with her father and grandparents. A small wooden rail served as a tether for all three horses.

"Maybe you should wait here. My grandparents are still sick," she reminded them. "I will just visit them for a few minutes and ask for the ointment. I will be right back."

The boys nodded, content to let their gazes fall across the village. Soon, a number of the Cree children caught up, and two of them chatted in a combined English and Cree while others stood by silently in their shyness.

The boys replied when they understood what was being said but soon concerned parents called their children back to their own homes. This freed John and Elmer to look around and take in their surroundings.

"Elmer, where have I seen that horse before? Doesn't it look familiar?" asked John, pointing to the distinctive horse in front of the chief's home.

Elmer stared inquisitively at the horse and then hesitantly stepped closer, as if to be sure of something about it. Then he spun around and looked right at John.

"John, that's Mr. Dumont's horse!"

***

Inside his home, Chief Five Hawks continued to study the young Métis man in front of him. The tall, dark haired stranger had sought a meeting with the chief a few days ago, introducing himself as the nephew of the great Gabriel Dumont. The chief had members of his council send him away while he considered the request. He never had the opportunity to meet Gabriel Dumont and yet, of course, his reputation as a remarkable warrior was legendary.

He knew that Gabriel Dumont had fought with all Native peoples, Indian and Métis alike, and that they shared many of the same concerns. The decline of the buffalo herds, the rapid spread of the European white people across the prairies, occupying land that once seemed unlimited—all this and more affected the original prairie dwellers.

At first, the Cree and other Indian tribes had welcomed the newcomers with open arms. But when their numbers grew and they began to populate the entire West, the buffalo disappeared from over-hunting. Then the white people came with their treaties and agreements, just when the Indian was hungry, the chief reflected. Chief Five Hawks was only a young man when the words of the white speaker were spoken aloud on that warm prairie day. But he remembered the hope he felt when he heard the message from the person they called the Queen, a distant ruler. He could still hear the man's voice, speaking on her behalf:

"The Queen Mother says, 'I hear that the natives are hungry at times. My arms are long; I shall uplift every one of my children. You will never again suffer for want of food. I shall distribute annually among all the natives a given sum of money… for as long as the sun will shine and the rivers flow. I have not come to buy your game nor the fishes in the lakes and streams; these are yours always. Three things only do I want, namely, the land which I will cultivate, also the timber, and the grass.'

"The Queen Mother says, 'I shall give to each head man a horse and carriage. I shall provide wise men and women to teach my children how to till the sod, and teach you the white man's way of making a living. I want all my people…to strive and get along with one another. I shall provide you with a strong-armed man. He of the Red Coat will protect you, fight for you and settle your difficulties. You will regard him as your brother.'"

Chief Five Hawks considered the trail of broken promises from the past. And what had he accomplished for his people of the Long River Band? What will be his legacy? What will he be remembered for? He managed business the best he could, but poverty was persistent. It seemed as if his legacy as chief would be marked only by indifference from a distant government. It seemed as if time had marched on and forgotten the Cree. He knew their allies, the Assiniboine, felt the same way. Chief Fallen Branch would surely be interested in what this young man had to say.

Then his thoughts turned to River's Voice, one of his own band members, now in jail on a murder charge that was surely not believable—another example of the white man's arrogance.

Yet, here was the nephew of Gabriel Dumont before him, with the spark of youth still lit and the energy to change things.

Was it possible to do more for his people? He felt the stirrings of hope again, not an easy feeling to activate in an old chief.

"You know your presence there would say a great deal," André said, as they walked outside under the morning sun. He stuck his hand out to shake and Chief Five Hawks accepted it.

"I will be there," the chief replied evenly, gripping the younger Métis man's hand firmly.

John and Elmer, who were hidden behind a shed, watched André Dumont and Chief Five Hawks shake hands.

"What did they say?" whispered Elmer.

"I don't know. I couldn't hear either," John said wonderingly.

"But I wish I knew why he was here."

With the ointment now in Summer's saddlebag, courtesy of her grandparents who were still feeling quite ill, the three travelers headed back to the Diefenbaker homestead. After getting briefed by John and Elmer, Summer didn't know what to make of André Dumont's visit either. But children were not permitted to know the plans or the ways of elders, or any adult either.

"We've got more important things to worry about anyway," said John. It had been two days since John's visit to River's Voice and he was feeling a sense of urgency to find out the truth of the murder of Hans Schneider. John tried to review the evidence against Summer's father, which included the necklace of River's Voice found near the scene of the crime.

"We know he had at least two arguments with Mr. Schneider in the past, going by what Sergeant English said," John stated. "Did you know about these, Summer?"

Summer nodded. "My father, he told me. One was a couple months ago, one just a while ago."

"What was it all about?" Elmer asked curiously.

"It was about not liking him because he is not white," said Summer quietly. "That's the way Mr. Schneider treated my father."

"Then why did he go back to Mr. Schneider's?" John tried to ask sensitively. "Why did he think it would be any different?"

Summer shrugged as her horse stepped over a gopher hole.

"I think my father wants to give everyone a chance. It's hard for him to understand why Mr. Schneider did not like him, just because he is Cree."

John understood what discrimination felt like, but in a different way. Sometimes the other children at school—the ones with English, Irish, and Scottish last names—made fun of his last name. 'Diefenbaker' reflected a German heritage and the name looked and sounded differently from his peers' family names. He also remembered the discrimination his black friends faced in Ontario when he was younger. Although he didn't remember all of the details, he remembered feeling a sense of unfairness on their behalf.

"The police have your father's necklace, found near the area where Mr. Schneider was…where everything happened," John said, not feeling like stating the obvious. "But I guess he could have lost it the last time he visited the Schneider farm to make a trade," John thought out loud.

Summer immediately agreed. "Yes, that is what must have happened."

"Did he tell you anything in particular that was said during the arguments, just in case there is some kind of clue we might have missed?" asked John.

"Clue?" asked Summer, not understanding.

"Yes, a clue is a helpful detail of some kind that might lead to a mystery being solved. It's like when police look for clues to solve a crime," John explained.

Summer shook her head and seemed downcast that she couldn't help more.

John continued to recap what they knew. "That's okay, Summer. There's more that we have to think about."

"Like what?" she asked.

"Like what happened to your father's pelts?" John asked, confused.

"Yes, how did Mr. Schneider find those?" Elmer questioned.

"It doesn't make any sense."

"Because he took them from us," said Summer accusingly. "Then he sold them and took our money."

John reined Skipper back a little, since the horse was starting to pull ahead too far. "Actually, all that we know for sure is that Mr. Schneider had your father's pelts and then he sold them. What we don't know is whether or not he took them. Plus we know that the Schneiders owed a lot of money to Mr. Taggart's general store."

"What? How do you know that?" Elmer asked.

John felt more like a detective now. "While you and Summer were looking around the store, I overheard Father and Mr. Taggart talking. Mr. Taggart mentioned that the Schneiders had a big debt with him and that he hoped Mrs. Schneider would be able to pay it off."

Elmer seemed excited now. "But then that means Mr. Schneider had a... a... what do the police call it, John?"

"A motive."

"Yes, he had a motive then, a reason for stealing the pelts!" said Elmer excitedly. "I agree with Summer. I think he did do it and you just helped prove it."

John wondered. "True, it does show he needed the money. It just doesn't seem like something Mr. Schneider would do, though."

John didn't say anything for a little while as the horses walked dutifully toward the homestead across the open prairies. Summer and Elmer fell silent, too, not wanting to break his train of thought. He had a new question for Summer.

"Did your father talk about the argument he had with Mr. Schneider in Borden? The police say they have witnesses who saw them arguing loudly and your father tried to take the pelts from his hands."

She shook her head. "No, he did not want to talk about it with me. I think he felt sad that all his work was wasted. He is a proud man and I think this was hard for him."

John straightened his back on Skipper and thought for a moment. "So, from the police's angle, they should realize both your father and Mr. Schneider needed money, then. I wonder if they know about the debt Mr. Schneider owed to Mr. Taggart at the store?"

"Good idea, John," said Elmer. "We should tell them!"

John wanted to move onto a new angle now and didn't reply to his brother.

"Summer, where did your father keep the pelts that were taken?"

"In our shed, behind the house. Father works to clean them and prepares them outside. Then, when they have been dried, he always puts them on a table in our shed."

"Was it locked?" asked John.

"No. We never lock it," she replied plainly. "We have not had anything stolen before."

"But still," said John, recapping, "that means Mr. Schneider would have had to travel five miles to the reservation, and for what reason? Could he have known there were pelts there to steal? I doubt it," said John, answering his own question. "And, he would have been recognized right away. He would have stood out."

"But then why would he bother going at all? Why would he take the time to travel there?" Elmer asked.

"Exactly," said John. "Maybe he didn't."

"But if he did not take them," said Summer, confused, "how did he get my father's pelts?"

John looked at Summer and Elmer. "That's what we need to figure out."

Chapter 10

Undercurrents

Rushing through Canada's Rocky Mountains, the powerful North Saskatchewan River flows easterly across Alberta and Saskatchewan before emptying into Lake Winnipeg in Manitoba. Many years ago European explorers traversed its swift-moving waters, looking for what they had not yet discovered and driven by what might be found. The river was still being used as a means of transportation for individuals and traders, just as the fur traders had done a hundred years earlier in the early 1800s. Many newcomer families and businesses established themselves along the shores of the river, where tiny villages and bustling towns formed into thriving prairie settlements.

At the sight of the majestic waterway, John, Elmer, and Summer pushed all thoughts of Chief Five Hawks and André Dumont from their minds. Each of them was eager to experience the refreshing coolness of the wide, swift river that carved through the thirsty fields.

John felt anxious as the three tied their horses to trees on the edge of the forest. All of the horses had already drunk their fill from the river and now they seemed content to stand in the shade.

Even the sight of so many trees in one area was a thrilling sight given their own land was fairly treeless back on the homestead. John wished he had time to explore the forest but the truth was he was nervous about even taking the time for a quick swim. It had always been more difficult for John to relax and have fun. He just seemed to be a natural worrier. In contrast, Elmer and Summer ran, splashing right into the river with their clothes on. No one was wearing shoes in the heat of summer and they knew their clothes would dry off as they galloped back to the homestead on their horses.

"Come on in, John!" Elmer yelled. "This is fantastic!"

Summer was already taking long, powerful strokes and when she surfaced she pointed to the middle of the river.

"Don't go there," she said. "See how the current moves the water? It's different there. It pulls the body, like this," she said, simulating someone being pulled under. She did it in such a funny and dramatic way she had Elmer in stitches and John laughing, too, as he slowly waded in.

Soon the anxiousness John was feeling evaporated and he began to enjoy the clean, bracing water that washed away his obligations. Even though he and Elmer were not great swimmers, it felt like they were able to fully enjoy themselves as they swam and floated in various spots along the river.

"Be careful…the current," Summer reminded them.

"We will," said John, as the brothers tried to push each other underneath the water, showing off in front of Summer. Soon, the boys found themselves in a full-fledged, water-based wrestling match. At one point, John was able to pick up Elmer, since the water made him lighter and more buoyant as part of his play-fighting. John staggered slightly from the weight of his brother. Before John could fix his footing, Elmer laughingly shifted his weight. As he escaped his older brother's grip, John felt himself stumbling backwards into the quick-flowing centre of the river.

He felt himself go under the water for a moment and thought it was just the momentum from wrestling with Elmer. As he pushed to break through to the surface again, he was only able to do this for a second as a strange, more powerful pull yanked him under the surface and then pushed him down the river with great force. It was a power like nothing John had ever experienced before.

As the river moved him around like a rag doll, carrying him farther along the middle of its wide girth, it would occasionally grant him a moment's frantic breath as he was yanked up and down, above and below the churning water. John was terrified and could no longer see where he had just been swimming.

Before he went under again he could hear the frantic screams of Summer and Elmer, who were running along the river bank, trying to keep up with him. When he bobbed up again, John felt he was imagining things. Each time he was pulled under the water then spit up again, he saw a different scene as the dominance of the river carried him along. At one point, with the bright sun and water in his eyes, he imagined he saw the shape of a man on a horse galloping beside him.

***

André Dumont listened again, stopping his powerful horse. Yes, there was no doubt that the voices he had been listening to had changed to screams. He impelled his large bronco to race toward the sound, the new pace exhilarating for the strong steed.

The forest path was a blur of greens and browns as horse and rider tore past the trees and the canopy of shade, into the strong light and beside a wide section of the river. To his left he quickly took in three horses standing by the edge of the forest near the river—a Pinto, and a light and darker brown pair of broncos. Farther down the river he could make out two children, a boy and a girl, running alongside the water, screaming. He clenched the sides of his horse firmly, demanding more speed as he moved faster toward them, his eyes scanning the currents of the river. Then he saw the bobbing head of another child, a boy, and directed his horse to run as close to the side of the river as possible. As soon as the horse drew past the flailing boy, Dumont slowed his stallion slightly and leaned sharply toward the river and jumped.

John didn't know what had grabbed him by the shirt, but he had no strength to resist. He could vaguely hear a voice, telling him that everything was fine and not to struggle. John was tired enough to be calm, and could feel himself being moved along on his back, his eyes squeezed shut because of the sun. Then John felt strong arms pull him out of the river and onto dry land where he was placed gently on the warm grass. He felt so thankful that the ground wasn't moving or pushing him any-where he didn't want to go. He loved it for its stillness.

The same hands that had dragged him now forced him onto his side, as water spewed out of his mouth and he could hear the voice of his brother and Summer, sounding worried and anxious. He could hear a man's voice, too, asking him to look at him, asking him to respond to his question. What was the question? It was so difficult to focus.

"John Diefenbaker, can you hear me?"

John slowly opened his eyes for the first time with full con-sciousness, staring up at a concerned-looking André Dumont. Elmer and Summer were leaning over him too, asking similar questions.

"I hate swimming," John finally said.

Elmer and Summer cheered and hugged him and Dumont offered him a hand to help him to his feet. John then lapsed into a coughing fit as his lungs forced out the remaining water.

The Métis man looked down at John with his blazing eyes from his full height, wiping his wet hair down so it was slicked back on his head. "This is a powerful river. You were very lucky," said André.

John nodded. "Thank you very much, Mr. Dumont. I don't know what happened."

"We were play wrestling and we got too close to the current and then…then all of a sudden you were gone," said Elmer, hanging his head. "I thought you were going to die."

John shook his head and assured his brother he was going to make it.

Elmer and Summer turned towards André. "Thank you for saving John," Summer said respectfully. "Oh, you're cut…on your arm," she said, pointing.

"It's nothing," dismissed André. "I did it on a rock when I jumped in. I'm sure it will heal just fine."

Summer offered him some of the ointment she had in her bag but he declined politely.

"If you are all well now, I shall take my leave."

John, Elmer, and Summer all thanked him.

John had a hundred questions for him as he watched, yet

there was only one thing that came out as André began to walk away.

"We saw you with Chief Five Hawks!" John blurted.

André stopped and slowly turned on his horse.

"What you saw was a meeting for freedom, for fairness. These are words Prime Minister Laurier knows nothing about, sitting in his tower in Ottawa," André said, bitterness creeping into his voice.

When he only heard silence, André spoke again.

"You will benefit in the end, all of you. I recall our last conversation, John Diefenbaker. Tell me, do you think the Cree are treated fairly…or the Métis?"

"Well, n-no," began John.

"Do you think it was fair to the Métis in the Battle of Batoche when they captured Louis Riel and drove my uncle into hiding in Montana?

"But…"

"And do you think it was fair that Poundmaker and Big Bear, two of the finest Cree leaders ever, were sentenced to prison terms when their main crime was starving at the hands of a government that could not care less?"

"No, but that was more than twenty years ago and…"

"Then what about right now, right here, John? Do you think it was fair that River's Voice had all thirty of his fox and beaver pelts stolen from his own shed, only to find out they're in someone else's barn? And then he gets accused of murdering the thief?"

"No, but…" started John.

"But what?" challenged André, slowly aiming the nose of his horse toward John, Summer and Elmer.

John remained silent.

"History lives, John. What you saw on the reservation was leadership in action. Compassion. There's change in the air. I hope you will be a part of it. Now go home and get some rest."

The well-toned bronco nodded its head a few times as if to indicate his impatience. André tipped his hat toward them, turned, and rode his horse deeply into the nearby woods. He was then out of sight, but not out of mind, of John, Elmer, and Summer.

***

They discussed what to tell Father and Mother on the way home. Elmer felt they should only mention having seen André Dumont at the reservation and admit to taking a quick dip in the river. John weighed everything in his mind. He considered Elmer's idea but his stomach immediately began to feel wracked with guilt at leaving out the major detail of almost drowning, and being saved by André. On the other hand, he would probably be grounded, forced to stay on the homestead for at least a week, if he told them everything. He likely would not even be allowed to ride Skipper. And then how would he help Summer's father?

"I think the bigger picture is to be able to help Summer's father," said John in conclusion. "So we should go with Elmer's idea…for now."

"Yes!" said Elmer, stabbing his fist into the air from atop Blue. The horse sighed as if annoyed from too much excitement.

"I said for now, Elmer. I don't feel right about not telling Father and Mother everything eventually. We need our freedom now in case we get some more clues to investigate," John explained. "We only have four days, remember, before…"

John's voice trailed off.

"Before my father is sent to trial," Summer finished. "You can say it, John. I know what will happen."

"I just have a feeling we're going to figure this out," said John. "Don't give up, Summer. We haven't."

***

"You did what? Did I just hear you say you went swimming… in the North Saskatchewan?" William asked in disbelief.

John nodded. Elmer and Summer were slightly behind John, looking at the ground.

Their clothes had essentially dried off from the long ride back, but it was still obvious from their wretched state they had been drenched in water.

"It's my fault. I was the one who made the decision," said John. "I wasn't thinking."

"You're darn right you weren't thinking. I have half a mind to ground you for the rest of the summer for a stunt like that."

Mary looked equally livid but bit her tongue while William spoke.

"As the eldest, you should have known better, John. The trip for you to Langham tomorrow is cancelled…"

"But …"

"Don't interrupt!" William said forcefully.

John knew his father was very angry because it was rare that he had ever seen him this upset. However, John was even more upset with himself. He should have known better and his parents were only concerned for their children's safety.

"You will stay home tomorrow and get some extra work done with me," said William, "while Elmer and Summer can go with Mary to help out."

"But you're both expected to do your share," he added, as Elmer and Summer nodded in agreement swiftly.

"Then all three of you can put some time in doing extra chores tomorrow as well," added Mary, anxious to contribute to the scolding.

John was disappointed about missing the trip to Langham, but he knew it could have been far worse. Right now he felt desperate for information that would save River's Voice and yet he didn't know where to turn. He only knew he had four days to help prove his innocence.

***

"Got any tonight, Mister?"

The train belched coal-fueled smoke into the dark night and groaned during its brief stop. A scowling, older rail engineer looked at the three boys in front of him, his grizzled features formed from a lifetime of hard travel along the railway.

"It's a bit late for you kids to be out, isn't it?" he snapped. "I'm busy. We're only in Borden for five minutes, then on to Prince Albert."

"Come on," said the tallest of the three boys. "We came all the way here to see them. We know this is the right train. My cousin works for the Canadian Northern Railway and he told me this is the train the prisoners always come in on. We've never seen real prisoners before."

"Yeah, well your cousin has a big mouth," said the engineer.

The boys didn't move, their eager faces staring up in anticipation.

"Fine," the engineer relented. "If it will get you kids out of here, let's get this over with. I've only got three tonight so there's not much of a show."

He muttered to himself as he picked up his lamp and marched over to a dark brown train car and grasped the metal lever. The boys followed close behind, so they could see clearly. With a heave the heavy door slid across. The old CPR worker stood there, arms crossed.

"Satisfied? Now can I get back to work?"

The boys blinked. "You mean you've only got two tonight, right, Mister?" said the same boy.

The engineer scowled. "What are you talking about, boy?" as he walked to their position to look into the train car. "If you're looking to provoke me tonight, it just might work."

For a moment the engineer was stunned. He shoved the lamp farther into the train car, as two blinking prisoners stared back. As he moved the lamp around, he could see the empty handcuffs hanging from the steel bar and began to shake his head slowly back and forth as the other two prisoners began to laugh menacingly.

"No, no...not him..." the old man said, looking terrified. Suddenly he grabbed the tallest kid by the shoulders and bent down to look at him closely, his frightened green eyes wild in the summer night.

"Run boy. All of you, run! And don't you stop until you reach home safely, you hear?" he warned fiercely.

The boys nodded, shocked, and ran as fast as they could, sneaking glances behind them at the old man.

"Breach! Breach!" the engineer screamed, running to find his colleagues on the train.

Chapter 11

The Warning of the Red Coats

"I thought we agreed you would stay out of sight," the tall man said sternly, standing beside a figure lying on his back near a fire pit. The tall man held a metal coffee mug and stared down into the dull embers.

"I have!" said the other man gruffly.

"Come on, how long have we known each other?" said the tall man. "Since school days! I know when you're lying. You were seen at Taggart's General Store. I have a source who confirmed this. You were also seen at the hotel at least once. We can't have this, you know. You've got to stay hidden."

The man on his back said nothing. A smear of white stars cast only a small amount of light. The moon, too, was weakened in its cycle. On the ground, only the dying coals of the latest fire barely pulsed. Otherwise the camp site was shrouded in darkness.

The taller man then picked up an object that he did not recognize.

"What is this? Did you steal this?"

"So what if I did?"

"Keeping items is not part of the plan. That is not what this is about!"

"Hey, I have to profit from this, too!"

The tall man shook his head. "Not this way. You can wait for success a little longer. And if you don't want to wait," said the tall man with an edge in his voice, "I will find someone who can."

The man lying down raised his head slightly. "You know, I know a few things about you, too."

The tall man extended his coffee mug and poured it onto the fading embers, extinguishing them. "And you will take them with you…to your grave."

***

There is an old prairie joke that says the land is so flat you can watch your dog run away from home for three days. Although that might be an exaggeration, there was no doubt it was fairly easy to see anyone approaching. With field after field of nothing but flat or gently sloping land, it was difficult to sneak up on anyone. That's why John, William, Ed and Elmer were not startled early the next morning at the sight of two Royal North West Mounted Police officers in their scarlet red tunics on horseback, coming up their laneway. They had watched them get closer for quite some time and worked until they arrived.

John wondered silently if they were here because of something to do with River's Voice. His heart felt like it was in his stomach as he kept working and thinking, trying to figure out other reasons they may be visiting again so soon. So much had been going on in such a short period of time he could barely process everything at once—their neighbour is murdered, their friend is imprisoned, a prairie fire almost destroyed their home and yesterday John almost drowned. Now, the police were visiting the homestead again, thought John.

"This better not delay getting to Langham," William muttered to Ed.

Ed nodded then replied, "It won't."

John couldn't picture anyone stopping his mother's butter sales plans, even though she couldn't go herself now. His mother had banged her leg on the woodpile last night, creating a painful bruise in the process. William had convinced her to stay home and let Ed be the butter salesman for today, while still taking Elmer and Summer with him for help. She didn't slow down for much, which meant that agreeing with this idea was a big deal for her. John would remain on the farm and help William out, while Mary would get some rest for her leg, if she could only agree to stay off of her feet and rest it. She knew that delaying the trip wasn't an option, or else the butter would spoil, and she certainly didn't want that to happen.

John was working alongside his father to mend a hole in the chicken coop while Elmer was helping Uncle Ed in the vegetable garden. Only Summer and Mary were in the house at this time preparing breakfast and didn't know the police officers were approaching.

Soon it was obvious that Sergeant English and Constable Wood were the visitors. Sergeant English was pointing his finger in a wide sweeping motion towards the blackened prairie area. Constable Wood was nodding. They seemed to be discussing the impact of the fire the Diefenbakers had narrowly escaped, thanks to a quick response and a lot of team effort.

William stood up straight and stretched his back, dropping his tools beside him.

"Good enough, John. We'll tend to this later."

"Mary!" yelled William when he had first seen them approach. "We've got company."

Mary appeared in the doorway. After taking one look at the two officers coming in the distance, she went into action, with Summer's help, preparing coffee for the arrivals.

"Yes, sir," said John, happy for the break and unsure of how he felt seeing the police. As the officers approached, John realized that this would be the perfect opportunity to make sure they knew about the big debt Hans Schneider owed to Max Taggart's store.

"Father," John said quickly. "I couldn't help but overhear you and Mr. Taggart talking about the debt Mr. Schneider owed to the general store. Do you think it's a good idea to see if the police know about it?"

William frowned at John. "Actually, I was already planning on telling them about it. I hope eavesdropping is not a regular pastime for you, either."

"No, sir, sorry Father," said John, relieved that the police would know about Mr. Schneider's debt.

When John heard the officers talking about the fire's path, he realized that perhaps they were simply here to check up on people in the area.

Ed and Elmer had already left the vegetable garden and were cleaning up. John could hear Elmer, trying to engage his mother in conversation when she was busy. That was his first mistake.

"Mother, the police are here!"

"Yes, I can see that Elmer, with the two eyes the good Lord gave me."

"Oh."

Choosing a new topic for the sake of conversation was his second mistake.

Mother, will we ever get a telephone?" asked Elmer.

"A telephone!" Mary snorted. "What are you thinking, boy? What do you think I'd need with a telephone, to do as much yakkin' as you do?"

"Well, I was thinking…"

"Can't say I believe you were thinking at all. Now, since you're here, full of ideas as usual, why don't you fetch me a basin of water. And don't spill any."

"Yes, Mother," said Elmer, sighing.

William, Ed and John walked closer to the officers, who were dismounting. They tied their horses to a makeshift tethering post near the barn and then greeted one another.

"From what we just saw," said Sergeant English, "it looks like you folks must have thought pretty quickly when the fire struck. Really glad to hear you're alright."

"Thank you," said William. "It was quite the battle. Any word on the extent of the damage?"

Constable Wood nodded. "Some. We're in the middle of checking it out for ourselves. Not everyone escaped as lucky, that's for sure."

"And how are you, young man?" asked Sergeant English to John.

For a split second John felt angry that the police were assessing fire damage when they should be figuring out who the real killer of Hans Schneider was. River's Voice was about to be shipped off to Regina in three days if the real murderer wasn't found. But then, of course they believed they already had the person who committed the murder. John felt stuck, with too little time to think and investigate. He wanted to solve this mystery before River's Voice was moved to Regina.

"I'm doing well, Sergeant English, thank you," John managed politely. "But did you know Uncle Ed burned his arm badly in the fire?" he asked, wondering why no one had brought this up yet.

"I was just about to ask about that bandage on your arm," said Sergeant English.

Ed shook his head. "It's nothing too much to be concerned about. Thanks to an ointment Summer got for me yesterday, it's doing a lot better.

John thought about the fact that Earl T. Wright had not stopped in yesterday to check on Uncle Ed and recommend a salve that would help, like he said he was going to do. That seemed strange—and it was right after he had lied about the contents in his wagon. Oh well, at least Summer had supplied an ointment.

"Yes, we heard the daughter of River's Voice is staying with you right now," said Sergeant English. "We need to speak with you for a few moments, if we may."

William turned to John.

"I want you, Elmer and Summer to go find something to do…outside," he said with emphasis. "Officers, would you like to come inside for some coffee?"

The police officers nodded while John and Elmer ran into the house to tell Summer. She followed the boys outside, looking warily at the officers.

The trio walked toward the barn a few paces, out of sight of the house. Once they couldn't be seen, John spun quickly.

"Let's go back and listen underneath the window. We might be able to get some more information." It suddenly occurred to John that eavesdropping actually was becoming a regular pastime. But how else was a kid supposed to get information?

Elmer looked thrilled with the idea. "That's a great idea, John, let's…"

"Elmer, there has to be no talking. We can't be caught. Let's hurry, and when I motion it's time to go, we move quickly. Got it?" John asked in a serious tone.

His younger brother and Summer both nodded and the three deftly scooted back towards the house, inching more slowly once they got closer. Finally, the three of them squatted underneath the kitchen window, which John knew had been open all morning. He held his hand to his lips as the sound of talking filtered through.

"…don't see why you wouldn't think it was a good idea to have her stay with us?" they heard William ask.

"Take it easy," said Sergeant English in his deep voice. "Look, we wanted to let you know there are a lot of folks out there who are getting kind of uneasy with the Cree and with the Indians in general."

"Why?" asked Ed.

"Ever since Hans was murdered and we arrested River's

Voice," began Sergeant English, "well, folks are angry that something like this could happen in a town the size of Borden."

"It didn't happen, that's the problem," said William.

The officers looked quizzical.

"The murder itself obviously happened," William continued, "but you've got the wrong man. River's Voice did not murder anyone."

Sergeant English made a sighing sound. "Look, his necklace, which he admitted was his, was found almost in the exact location where the murder was committed. He was in two heated arguments with the deceased and we have Kyle and Isabelle Jennings saying they witnessed River's Voice utter a death threat to Hans Schneider when they were arguing in Borden over pelts. You may not think that's enough evidence but men have gone to jail and stayed there with less evidence than that sometimes."

Summer clapped her hand over her mouth to stop from crying out. John and Elmer looked at her and hoped she could continue to listen. On a positive note, John believed that he had just overheard a clue to follow up on that he didn't have before. He now knew who witnessed Hans Schneider and River's Voice arguing—the Jennings.

"The bottom line is there's a new level of distrust out there right now," said the sergeant. "We just want you to watch your back. People can be irrational."

John, Elmer, and Summer crowded in to listen, but there seemed to be an awkward silence. They heard Mary ask about more coffee and the sergeant politely decline. Then they heard Constable Wood.

"Some are even saying this fire was set by the Cree in retaliation for the arrest of River's Voice."

"That's crazy," said Ed. "I don't believe it for a minute."

Summer looked at John and Elmer with disbelief, too.

Constable Wood spoke with a calming voice. "But this is the way things are now. It seems as if this tragedy involving your neighbour has stirred up a lot of tensions. We heard the fire hit the Coulter family pretty hard two farms north of you and Karl Petersen lost about a third of his crop. I don't know what old Karl thinks, but the Coulters think the Cree are striking back because we arrested River's Voice."

"There was a thunderstorm all that night," said William, exasperated. John knew he had shifted his chair because he could hear it slide across the floor. "Any fool could tell it was obviously because of a lightning strike."

"It's not all rational," reminded the constable.

"Poor old Karl," said Mary quietly, who was thinking about how often he had helped out the Diefenbakers with the water difficulties they were having. "We must get over there and see how he's doing," she said to William.

William mumbled agreement, but John could tell he was

clearly distracted.

"Speaking of tensions," began Sergeant English, who then stopped in mid-sentence. He brought his mug of coffee to his lips and slurped it loudly enough for the three to hear it outside.

"We know for a fact that André Dumont had a meeting with Chief Five Hawks, just yesterday. I mention this because you just said your children were there at the reservation yesterday, too."

John, Elmer, and Summer all looked at one another. They were surprised the police already knew.

"The boys were there yesterday with Summer to get Ed the ointment for his arm. They mentioned they noticed him there but I don't think they made contact. Why do you think he was there?" asked William.

John tried to lean in more closely, although he was right against the outside of the house already and his ear was likely going to get a sliver from the wooden wall. Elmer was leaning onto his foot at the same time, which was additionally irritating.

"We wish we knew," said Sergeant English. "Our sources were not able to confirm. But given that he fancies himself as carrying on his famous uncle's work, he's been pretty busy trying to stir things up against the government. He's been careful. We can't charge him on anything yet. But if I was Laurier, I'd be keeping my eye on what's happening around here lately."

"The prime minister?" William asked in disbelief. "Are you that worried that something is going to happen?"

"Hard to say which way the pendulum will swing. All I'm saying is I've let the Prime Minister's Office know what's going on around here," said the sergeant with some self-importance. "We have our ear to the ground and if something breaks, we'll be ready."

There was some shuffling of cups and then Ed spoke.

"From everything you've said, doesn't Dumont benefit the most from the tension going on? Did you ever think of him for the murder of Hans Schneider?"

John had mixed feelings about his uncle's statement. What he said made sense, but on the other hand he was beginning to like André Dumont. And twice, now, André had saved John.

"Of course," said the sergeant. "With him being new in town, he was one of the first people we wondered about. First, we wanted to check out his story to make sure he is who he says he is, the nephew of Gabriel Dumont. He claims his father was Joseph Dumont. Well, I never heard of him but I checked with a few Métis sources and they tell me Gabriel did have a younger brother named Joseph, although they weren't very close.

"But what about his whereabouts on the night of the murder?" asked Ed.

"It wasn't him," said Sergeant English. "That's why I didn't look into it any more deeply. His alibi was air-tight. He was sitting in a hotel having a drink and there were eight other men and the barmaid who can vouch for him during the time of the murder."

Mary made a scoffing sound at the mention of alcohol again. It was something of a reflex for her. John was almost relieved that Mr. Dumont could account for where he was on the night of the murder, with witnesses.

William finally mentioned what John had been waiting for. "Did you know that Hans Schneider had a big debt with Max Taggart?"

"As a matter of fact," said Sergeant English, "we are aware of that."

"Well, doesn't that point to Hans, as much as I hate to say it, more than it points to River's Voice?" William added. "Maybe he did take those pelts to sell to help clear his debts?"

John was happy his father was pressing this.

Sergeant English slurped some of his coffee again and set the mug down with a clunk before replying. "William, it doesn't add up. That would mean Hans knew there were pelts waiting to be taken, knew precisely where River's Voice lived and then knew where they were being stored. Not to mention the fact that he wasn't a young man and would have difficulty stealing all those in one trip. Believe me, we've thought of these things."

John realized the sergeant was right—some of what he had

said he had already discussed with Elmer and Summer.

"Anyways, folks," said Sergeant English.

Were they about to leave? John touched Elmer and Summer on the arm to tell them to scramble around the corner of the house if it sounded like they were leaving.

The sergeant's voice carried on. "We just wanted to let you all know there have been a few break-ins lately, too. It's getting serious enough that we've already got a few reinforcements on their way to help us investigate. This town's been busier than a gold rush lately."

"I suppose people in town are blaming the Indians for these break-ins, too?" asked William sarcastically.

"I'm sure some are," said Sergeant English.

"Sorry to have to rush off," said Ed, sliding his chair back. "But I've got plans to get into Langham this morning. We've got a lot of butter to load up yet, too."

"That's quite alright," said Sergeant English. "We've got to move along anyway. You folks take care—Mary, thanks for the coffee—and good luck with those butter sales."

John gave a frantic 'go' signal with his index finger to his brother and Summer. They couldn't get caught listening in so soon after getting in trouble for being at the river or they'd never leave the homestead until they were adults. They scrambled quickly around the corner of the house, with Elmer rolling in the dirt for dramatic effect in his getaway. They kept on going to the barn then whirled around as if they were just exiting the barn after visiting the animals. John, Summer and Elmer walked back and stood beside the adults.

As the two police officers walked outside and prepared to mount their horses, Constable Wood turned to face Summer.

"It's the strangest thing. Whenever we leave the station, your father begins to sing."

Summer broke into a wide grin, which the young Mountie noticed.

"Do you know why that might be?" asked Constable Wood.

She nodded.

"Yes. It means that my father is keeping his word to the elders. It means that he will not give up."

Chapter 12

The Butter Trail

Mary Diefenbaker liked to sell her own butter, thank you very much. After all, it was her hard work—with churning assistance from John and Elmer sometimes—that made these butter-selling trips even possible. She surveyed the work of the rest of the family, knowing this time she wouldn't be a part of the action because of her leg. It was a disappointment, but that was life, wasn't it?

When they lived in Fort Carlton, she used to sell it in nearby Rosthern, a major trading town. Since moving to the Borden area, the Diefenbakers mainly did local trading and selling, but they preferred the butter market in farther-away Langham where Mary had more regular customers. The trip to Langham was about eleven miles but at least Mary could usually count on selling for a good price. All in all, the butter sales were a helpful source of additional income for the family. Sometimes the family used the butter for barter, such as with old Karl to trade for fresh water. And sometimes they traded butter in the stores when they wanted other foods, such as canned fruits and vegetables that were difficult to grow on the prairies.

Butter-making was an art, no doubt about it. At first, Mary had to skim the cream from the surface of the milk and allow it to set in pails. If she could keep John away from the buttermilk—that is, from drinking down some of the profits—she sometimes sold this, too. Then the cream was placed in the churn and the handle turned until the butter became the desired consistency. The Diefenbakers used a combination of wooden pails that could hold five pounds of butter and wooden tubs that could carry larger amounts. Some stores liked to have the butter pre-made into rolls so Mary also took the time to package it in various ways to increase her sales.

William and John helped Ed, Elmer, and Summer load the wagon with the tubs and pails of butter and everything was checked twice before their departure. Skipper and Blue had already been hitched up and the team was ready for the long trip to Langham. William requested a *Langham Times* newspaper to catch up on the latest politics and local news.

John gave Elmer and Summer a wish-I-was-going-too look before they boarded the wagon. He might not be able to go to Langham, John thought to himself, but at least it would give him some time to talk with his father. Time was ticking by for River's Voice and John had a lot of questions and very few answers.

***

As Skipper and Blue plodded along the road, Elmer and Summer forgot they would have to cross the great bridge that spanned the North Saskatchewan River to get to Langham. They gulped as they were half way across the river, remembering the watery ordeal John had gone through only a day earlier. Once across the bridge, there were a few more miles of the typical flat landscape and then Ed, Elmer and Summer finally began to see the distinct shapes of buildings in the distance.

Langham was small yet bustling with activity and, like Borden, was prospering thanks to the establishment of the Canadian Northern Railway a few years ago. The train line ran all the way to Edmonton, Alberta, moving people across the West to some of the more northern towns and cities with a reliability that used to be lacking. Langham was a diverse town, made up of European settlers, Doukhobor families from Russia, and Mennonite settlers who had emigrated from the United States.

As the wagon made its way along the main street, Ed steered past the Langham Bruderthaler Mennonite Church, reading the various business signs until he found the general store that he knew Mary liked to deal with.

While Ed jumped down to negotiate with the store owner,

Elmer and Summer also got down and took in the bustling town with a sweep of their eyes. There were people buying and selling all kinds of goods down the main road, including dry goods, soap, small animals like geese and chickens, and building materials—all manner of bartering and buying that one could imagine.

"The town seems busy today," said Elmer. "I haven't been here in a long time."

"And I have never been here," noted Summer, looking around. "I like it. It seems like Borden."

A black youth, perhaps sixteen or seventeen years old, who had been walking by, suddenly stopped and looked at them.

"You're from Borden?" he asked.

Elmer and Summer both nodded.

The youth grinned. He was dressed in drab, worn clothing but had a twinkle in his eye. He was about average height and carried a small satchel with him, which they assumed contained his personal belongings. The satchel he carried gave him the look of someone who was travelling.

"The railway goes through Borden, too. Isn't that right?"

"Yes," Elmer said. "Are you going on a trip further west?"

The youth puffed out his chest some. "I'm hoping to find work on the railway. No luck so far," he said, glancing around with disappointment. Then he added, "I'm Matthew Carver."

Elmer and Summer introduced themselves. Elmer had never

spoken to anyone who was black before, at least not in the West and not for many years. Back in Ontario, he had vague memories of playing with black friends, although John remembered better because he was older.

By this time, Ed had noticed they were chatting with the teenager and stared for a little bit until he decided all was well. He then continued negotiating with the store owner.

"Where are you from, Matthew?" Elmer asked in a conversational way.

"Rosetown, southwest of here," he replied. "My family came here from Oklahoma a year ago. We heard about the free land. Takes a while to get the land working properly, though, doesn't it?"

Elmer nodded. He relayed the struggles with their own family's homestead north of Borden and Summer talked about life on the reservation and how her father turned to trapping for most of their income because of the difficulty he had farming.

"Trapping? That sounds exciting," said Matthew enthusiastically. "I wish I knew how to do that. I'm not sure I like the part about killing animals, though."

Elmer and Summer laughed. He grinned and then seemed to be thinking about something else.

"Wasn't there a murder in Borden recently? I heard they caught the person who did it. Actually, I heard he was Cree, like you," Matthew said, not realizing the connection.

"My father did not do that. He's innocent!" said Summer.

"Your father!" exclaimed the youth. "Oh!"

Elmer explained the whole story to Matthew.

"You were there?" he said impressed. "That's incredible, Summer, I do hope they find the real killer, now that I know your father didn't do it. It's a terrible thing when someone makes up their mind about you, especially when they don't even know you."

Summer and Elmer studied his face and wondered if Matthew was also talking about his own experiences with being misjudged. It was quiet for a few awkward seconds until Elmer switched subjects.

"Is working on the railway the only kind of work you want to do?"

Matthew studied the ground near his feet. "I'd take any job, really but most places aren't willing to hire someone like me."

Summer nodded. "You mean…because your skin is dark?" she said, rubbing her own skin on her arm to make her point.

He shook his head in agreement. "But railways will sometimes hire black people, as porters and baggage handlers. I've seen it with my own eyes," he said, trying to stay positive.

"Where do you live when it's winter?" asked Elmer, wondering about his travelling lifestyle.

"Well, I've always lived with my family, with my parents and two younger sisters. We've only had one winter here. It's

155

not something I look forward to seeing again, no sir-ee," he said with seriousness. "It's a lot different in Oklahoma, that's for sure."

His body seemed to experience a chill, even though the hot August sun beat down.

"Where will I live? I don't know." Matthew looked distant. "I need a job and then a place of my own, I expect. You ever wish you could see what life has in store for you?" he asked. He didn't wait for an answer.

"I do," Matthew continued quickly. "But that's what happens when you get older," he said, his chest swelling again. "You start wondering about your future."

Elmer nodded in a good natured way and then there was more silence before Matthew spoke again.

"Hey, what are you doing in Langham anyway?"

"Selling butter," said Elmer, jabbing his thumb toward his uncle. "My Uncle Ed is selling it here for my mother. Then we have to pick up some supplies and a newspaper for my father and head back."

"Oh, I thought you might have come to hear what that fellow has to say…what's his name…Dumont?"

Elmer dropped his jaw.

"Dumont? André Dumont?"

***

Back at the homestead, William was trying to convince Mary that resting her leg while working in the henhouse was not really resting her leg at all. The sound of an approaching wagon interrupted the discussion. William soon found himself greeting Harold Devonshire, one of the Diefenbaker's neighbours on the north side of their property. John, who had been working in the garden, approached the visitor, too, when his father waved him over.

"Hello, William, Mary. Hello, John, hello," said the Englishman, removing his hat temporarily while he greeted the Diefenbakers. Harold, who was tall and thin with equally thin hair, liked to repeat most things twice, if not more. Having just arrived from England two years ago, his English accent was unmistakable.

"Harold, how have you and Margaret been?" asked William.

"We've been meaning to come by to see how you coped with the fire."

"Ahh, not good, not good" he said. "We lost nearly half, I'm afraid. Nearly half."

"Oh, Harold," said Mary sympathetically, putting her hands to her mouth in shock. "We're sorry to hear that. Is there anything we can do for you? And so close to the harvest!"

"No, no. We're alright. I thank the Lord last year was a good crop. We're going to make it, though I know it won't be an easy year. It won't be easy but we'll do it."

"Coffee?" William asked.

"No, thank you. I'm here on other business. I just wanted to ask if your farm was broken into. Anything stolen…stolen at all?"

"No, but the police were here just this morning warning us there had been more than the average number of break-ins. Why? Don't tell me you were robbed, too?" asked William.

Harold nodded. "Oh yes, yes sir. Lost all of our canned goods we had stored. I'm just on my way into Borden now to replace a few things…a few things, anyway."

William and Mary offered some of their own canned goods, but Harold politely declined.

"And it's not just me, that's the thing," Harold went on. "Karl Petersen had his watch taken that his late wife had bought for him…"

"Not Karl, too!" said Mary.

"…and Otto and Justina Kowalski had their savings stolen from under their bed. Last week, Nicholas and Liza Petrenko had some family heirlooms taken. In fact, for whatever reason, it seems like your house is the only one that hasn't been robbed in the area lately, at least as far as I can tell. The only one. Why is that, I wonder?" asked Harold.

John, who had been listening with disbelief, wondered why, too. William and Mary were still reeling from all the news that had affected their neighbours.

"Well, I have no idea, I…" began William.

"If the timing was different, I'd be blaming it on the escaped convict. But that only happened last night," Harold interrupted.

"What escaped convict?" asked Mary, apprehensively.

"You didn't hear? Last night, the prisoner transport car? Some big-time murderer escaped. They say he's from Winnipeg, Winnipeg, they say. Anyhow, I would have blamed him for the thefts, too, except most of these break-ins happened before."

"This is incredible," said William, hardly believing the level of chaos that was occurring lately.

"People are upset," said Harold, clearly getting more agitated. Old Hans is murdered next door to you. Then we have to deal with fire that destroys our crops…except yours, I hear?

"We were lucky…" Mary started to explain.

"Ploughed the furrows in time…" finished William.

"Lucky indeed," said Harold. "On top of murders and fires, now folks' homes are being robbed from under our noses. I mean, what kind of country is this? What kind?"

William and Mary had never seen Harold so upset, but he seemed to have good reason to be.

"We need some changes around here, that's what I say," he said, climbing back onto his wagon. He said 'changes' with a strange gleam in his eye. "Some folks are ready to try and make that happen."

"Now, what do you mean by that?" asked William.

"Oh, nothing, I guess," Harold replied. "Just talk. Just talk. I better get into town. Bye now."

Harold signalled his horses to begin moving, nodding at the Diefenbakers as he turned the animals toward Borden.

Chapter 13

'Maybe Dumont is Right'

Elmer was obviously surprised, but Matthew Carver didn't know why.

"Yes, André Dumont. That's him. Why, do you know this Dumont fellow?" asked Matthew.

"We've met before," said Elmer, looking at Summer. Elmer snuck a glance at his uncle who was still deep in conversation with the store owner.

"Well, he's all done talking now, anyway, so I was going to let you know you missed it. He finished up about three-quarters of an hour ago."

"What did he talk about?" asked Summer.

Matthew lifted his hat and scratched his head. "Well, that man can really speak, I tell you. He had nearly twenty people gathered around, even though there were only five or six at first. He was telling folks what's wrong with the West, for the Métis, the Indians, and settlers. He even mentioned people of colour, like me. I think I like him," Matthew concluded.

"That's what he does in Borden!" Elmer exclaimed. "We have to tell John," he said to Summer.

"Who's John?" asked Matthew.

"Our big brother…er, my big brother," said Elmer.

"Well, tell him he can still catch the big rally. It's not like he won't have another chance to hear him," said Matthew.

Elmer and Summer scrunched their foreheads.

"Big rally?" Summer asked, unsure of the word.

Matthew nodded. "Yeah, you know, a big get-together. It's tomorrow. He invited everyone to come and show support for the cause. It's going to be on some farm… what did he say now …oh, yeah… the Petrenko farm. One hour after sundown."

"Petrenko? Mr. Petrenko's farm isn't very far from ours!" said Elmer, scarcely believing his ears.

"Really? I think it's going to be a whopper. He said people were coming from all over the area. He said it was time to take back the West for everyone. It sounded good to me, but I'm not really sure what that means, mind you. I'm surprised you didn't know about the rally since you live nearby."

"Me, too," said Elmer simply.

Ed, having concluded his transaction, turned toward Elmer and Summer and motioned them over to the wagon where he wanted to get the butter unloaded for the store owner who was waiting.

Elmer and Summer said they had to go, pivoting their feet in the direction of Ed. "It was nice meeting you, Matthew!" called out Elmer.

"Good luck looking for a job!" shouted Summer.

Matthew waved back and smiled. "Thanks, maybe I'll see you around again sometime!"

Once Ed, Elmer, and Summer unloaded the wooden pails and tubs, the butter then had to be transferred to the store owner's own storage containers. The small packages Mary had prepared were fine as they were. Soon the store owner was counting out money for Ed and they shook hands. Ed grimaced slightly, still feeling some pain in his arm that had been burned in the fire. He put it out of his mind as he used some of the new money to get the few things Mary had requested for him to pick up in the store.

Elmer and Summer showed interest in looking around the general store, although it wasn't as well stocked as Taggart's in Borden, they decided.

"Uncle Ed, can we pick up the newspaper for Father?" Elmer asked. "The *Langham Times* building is just across the street," he said, pointing through the open doorway.

Ed considered the request. "I guess so," and handed him a coin. "Make sure you get the most current one," he said.

Elmer and Summer sprinted for the door.

"Oh, Elmer!" called Ed.

"Yes, Uncle Ed?"

"Take your time but hurry back," he replied, then let out a high-pitched laugh.

Elmer groaned. His uncle always had the same jokes.

Across the street the small office of the *Langham Times* looked like it had been built on an angle, giving it a decrepit look. Elmer picked up a newspaper on the counter and handed the man a ten cent piece. The man returned five cents to him and Elmer slipped it into his pocket, as he and Summer looked at the cover and exited onto the street. Summer's ability to read English was not as strong as her ability to speak it, so she asked Elmer to read the headlines to her.

One of the main newspaper headlines read '*Federal Election Likely This Fall.*' A sub-head underneath read '*Laurier Under Pressure Across Canada.*'

"Wow, an election might happen soon," said Elmer. "That will get everyone talking. I can't wait to tell John about Mr. Dumont, too, and…

Summer thumped Elmer on the arm. "Look! Over by the blacksmith shop," she said, pulling Elmer behind a parked wagon.

It was Earl T. Wright's unmistakable canary yellow wagon. There was Earl, standing in front of it, speaking to André Dumont.

***

The night had been sleepless and anxious. Might this be the price of revenge? Actually, he didn't care because he now knew that this was the area where his quarry often made his travels. The one he sought had been spotted frequently north of Borden lately. Soon he would find him and the wait would be worth it.

The warm sun shone on his grizzled features. His wrists still ached from the handcuffs from last night's escape and he rubbed them gingerly. For now, he would camp near this abandoned shack he had found on the edge of Borden. Soon a wagon would eventually move northward and he would ride it without detection. When the time was right, he would make his move.

***

"What are they doing?" he whispered hoarsely to Summer. "At Mr. Schneider's funeral, Mr. Wright said he was worried about André Dumont. He said he was dangerous. Now he's chatting with him? We have to get closer."

Elmer and Summer navigated deftly between wagons parked in front of the various businesses, ensuring they were not seen. André and Earl were standing near a business that boasted a large porch with many shrubs and flowers, which provided effective cover for Elmer and Summer to listen.

"…I liked Hans, but, as I said, he surprised me. But enough about that. What do you need from me if I agree to this?"

"Just show up, for now," André replied. "Just be there, lend your support, and I won't ask much more of you, other than the odd message delivered here and there."

Elmer and Summer looked at one another. She glanced back to see that Ed had just walked out of the store. She tapped Elmer on the arm and pointed, wide-eyed, to Ed.

Ed walked toward the wagon and quickly surveyed the main street, looking for Elmer and Summer. They abruptly appeared from behind a wagon only a few strides away.

"And just what are you two doing?" asked Ed.

Elmer held up the newspaper. "Just got the *Langham Times*, Uncle Ed."

"From behind a wagon?" he asked, challenging the answer.

"We were pretending we were reporters. We were investigating," he said sheepishly.

Summer chose to simply nod and look at the ground.

Ed peered at them with curiosity. "Well now, that's great… reporters. And right now you're both going to be in new careers. I call it manual labour. Let's get all of this packed up and then back home we go."

"Yes, Uncle Ed," as they snickered quietly over Ed's joke.

***

Back in Borden, the front door of the Royal North West Mounted Police office closed and a visitor shuffled away.

"What did you make of that old Métis man, Sergeant? Think there's something there to investigate?" Constable Wood bent his tall, well-toned frame over to peer outside the small window of the police office, watching the old man hobble away until he reached his equally tired-looking horse.

Sergeant English sat up rigidly in his desk chair, tugging his scarlet red uniform downward to get rid of stray wrinkles.

"We've got enough to do with this train escape, that's for sure. Those reinforcements can't get here soon enough to help conduct a proper search."

"So you don't want me to bother?" replied the younger officer.

"I didn't say that," Sergeant English said harshly. "You follow up on every lead that comes your way, Constable. Every one of them. Now get on that new-fangled phone to Regina or Winnipeg to get some decent answers."

"Yes, sir."

***

John wiped the sweat from his forehead with his arm and leaned briefly on the shovel he had just been using. The sun was relentless, other than the brief mercy of a few white clouds. They passed in front of the sun for only a minute or two, their fleeting nature exposed by warm prairie winds.

He kicked a weed he had been about to dig up. It wasn't as

effective as using the shovel but it sure felt better, John decided.

He glanced toward the homestead and saw his mother peer out at him through the small window. He wondered if she had seen him kick the weed. She didn't come out and holler at him, so that was a good sign John decided.

The battle of weeds and vegetables being waged in the Diefenbaker garden didn't seem nearly as important as the battle being waged in John's head. How could he have gotten himself grounded at the homestead? It was a stupid decision, he thought harshly, to go swimming at a time when he needed to be able to count on what little freedom he had. He had only three days left until River's Voice was transferred and here he was, pulling weeds like there was nothing wrong. John felt hemmed in by his own life.

William came from the barn where he had been making a repair to Lily's cow stall. His eyes quickly combed over the work John had been doing to make certain reasonable progress had been made. John hoped his father didn't say he missed any weeds. He hated retracing his steps when it came to getting work completed. John always tried to do it right the first time so he wouldn't have to do it again.

"Looking good, John," said his father simply, stuffing a sweaty rag into his overalls after wiping his face.

John nodded, quietly happy about the answer. Maybe this was a good time to ask a few questions that had been simmering in the back of his mind. Asking his father questions came naturally for John, especially since William was also his teacher.

"Father, what will happen to Summer if River's Voice is... well, if he's found guilty and sent to jail...forever?

William looked off into the distance, gathering his thoughts.

"It's not an easy thing to answer, John. My guess is that she would continue to live on the reservation, with her grandparents and the rest of her Cree band," he said. "Hopefully they will get feeling better soon."

"What's wrong with them?" John asked.

"From what I've heard, it's influenza."

"Isn't that what Mrs. Braithwaite died of last year? What if they don't get better? Then what?"

"I can't answer for sure, John," said his father. "Sometimes we have to see what life brings us. I know that there are other relatives on the reservation who will step in and help."

John attempted to dig another weed in front of his father, but somehow it didn't work. That always seemed to happen. Whenever his father was watching he couldn't seem to do something perfectly, even if he knew how to do it when he wasn't being watched. His father reached out for the shovel, obviously wanting to demonstrate. John sighed.

"You need to get a better angle with the shovel...like this," he said. The high puff of hair on his father's head shook back and forth when he pushed the shovel into the dirt.

John nodded, pretending to need the lesson when all he needed was his father not to be looking at him. He decided to ask another question while William was still beside him.

"Why do Indians live on reservations?"

"Now why do you ask that, son?" his father said, shoveling another weed onto a pile John had already started.

John shrugged slightly. "I mean I remember some of this from history but I still don't understand it completely. Why can't they just live however they want to live?"

William gave a grunt of understanding. "Good question, and there are many answers. Let's put one of the big answers this way."

"Before the West started to attract more Europeans, there weren't many people here, other than the Indians. So you should think of the Indians as the first nation. There were also fur traders who made their living along the rivers and lakes. But the people from eastern Canada, Ontario, Quebec, and the Maritime provinces, believed in owning land. So did the people who came here from Europe, which is the majority of us. For them, it didn't make sense not to have boundaries and rules set up."

John understood. "So the Indian idea of sharing land was something we didn't really understand. We still don't get it."

William nodded.

"So you mean people like us," John stated.

"Yes, people like us, son. It's difficult to admit but in some ways it's true. It's a clash of cultures, John. Not to mention the buffalo were overhunted and almost became extinct. The government came in and offered food, shelter, and training in farming. It was trying to help in its own way, but the government also wanted access to these prairies for the newcomers," said William, waving his hand at the golden wheat.

John took the shovel back from his father. "I think I understand why the Cree and other Indian tribes are disappointed. They have to live on reservations and don't have the freedom to move around wherever they want," said John. "But what about the Métis? Why are so many Métis angry, like Mr. Dumont? They're not all stuck on reservations."

"I can't speak for this Dumont fellow, John. But the traditional Métis buffalo hunts were affected once the buffalo was driven away and overhunted. They're still not free to move around if the government — and then the settlers — are claiming to own the land they used to hunt on."

"It was the Americans who overhunted the buffalo, right?" John asked.

"They weren't the only ones overhunting. But yes, since their West was settled first there were a lot of Americans involved in the hunt," said William, "and buffalo have no borders."

"They would cross back and forth between Canada and the U.S. all the time. The Métis loved to be a part of this lifestyle, too, and then all of a sudden it was gone. And neither the Indians nor the Métis were anxious to be absorbed by a government that didn't understand the way they wanted to live," said William.

"It doesn't sound like anyone is really happy," noted John.

His father laughed. "It sure seems that way. When you think about it, white settlers were often ignored by the government, too. The government's main interest was to simply get the people out here farming. That's all they've cared about, as far as the West goes. How can we get them here and get the country growing?"

"So maybe Mr. Dumont is right, then," John stated. He was feeling more heated about the issues the West had been dealing with. "The Métis are driven away from their lifestyle by settlers, the Indians are forced to live on reservations and take help from the government because their lifestyle is taken away, and maybe they get blamed for doing things they didn't even do, like River's Voice and…"

"John…" began his father.

"…and we, we don't even get fair prices for our wheat each year!" said John, his voice rising. He was still on a roll.

"Sergeant English said Mr. Dumont is whipping up emotions in people, but that's because they have a right to feel the way they do. We need to be emotional about these things, don't we, Father?"

William pulled his rag from his pocket and wiped his face again. He stared at his eldest son, with a mixture of admiration and caution.

"I guess that all depends on what we do with our emotions, doesn't it, son?"

With that William ambled into the homestead and left John alone with his shovel and his swirling thoughts. Now he could no longer simply concentrate on the dilemma of River's Voice, like he had wanted to do. Instead, he began to consider the condition of all of his neighbours' lives—whether Indian, Métis or settlers—who felt like they didn't have a say. It was as if all the underdogs of the Canadian West seemed to haunt John and weigh heavily on his mind. He felt like an outsider within his own country.

He aimed his shovel at another large, invading weed and severed it at the root.

**

Returning over the great bridge that spanned the North Saskatchewan River didn't seem quite as upsetting this time to Elmer and Summer. But as the wagon creaked along toward home on the well-worn road, there were new fears to replace it.

Elmer and Summer were uneasy about Earl's comments, and they also wondered about André's rally on the Petrenko farm and what that would mean. This added a strange twist to a visit to Langham that was only supposed to have been about butter. They wanted to get back home to the Diefenbaker homestead to let John know as soon as possible.

They felt the wagon turn to travel north of Borden on a familiar-feeling trail and could see the town's recognizable buildings in the distance to the west. The wagon path that headed north of Borden and back toward the homestead was a creaky, noisy ride. The smaller path was not nearly as well-worn as the one that connected the towns together. As they passed by a familiar shack, long ago abandoned by a settler who never made it, Ed thought he heard a dull thump of some kind.

"Did either of you stomp?" Ed asked.

"No, not us," said Elmer, who was seated right behind his uncle in the back row of the front of the wagon. Summer sat beside him and shook her head.

"Maybe a barrel fell over," said Elmer. "I'll look."

Elmer twisted around and peered into the darkened back of the wagon, which was covered by the canopy. He moved aside one flap and peered in, but all he could see were barrels, and all of them were standing.

"Everything's fine, Uncle Ed."

Ed nodded, his face furrowed, making a mental note to check the condition of the wheels back at the homestead.

***

He felt cramped inside the back of the wagon, but the barrels were the perfect cover for him. He would jump off once he felt he was far enough north of Borden. It was time for a payback as soon as he could pin down his target. If he really thought that by staying on the move he could avoid his fate, he was sorely mistaken.

Chapter 14

'We Will Take Back the West'

Constable Wood hung up the telephone gingerly, afraid to break it. Like many others, he was still in awe of the technology.

"You're not going to believe this, Sergeant, but they know each other."

"Tell me everything," said Sergeant English.

After hearing the young constable's full report, Sergeant English smoothed his thick brown moustache, deep in thought.

So much had just changed. The best way to handle the situation was to let events unfold naturally. Then, hopefully, they could clean up this town once and for all.

***

"He said what?" asked John.

Elmer and Summer were now back at the homestead and the trio of youngsters had more to talk about than they would have imagined. Elmer repeated exactly what they heard, from Earl's strange comments to André's plans for the following night.

"Mr. Wright said 'I liked Hans, but, as I said, he surprised me. But enough about that. What do you need from me if I agree to this?'"

"That's exactly what he said?" asked John, concerned.

Elmer nodded. John looked paler than usual.

"Then Mr. Dumont replied 'Just show up for now. Just be there, lend your support, and I won't ask much more of you, other than the odd message delivered here and there.'"

John replayed this over and over in his mind, looking for alternative explanations. But no other explanation came to him. Somehow Earl T. Wright was surprised by Hans being out in the field. That had to be what the Rawleigh's man meant, figured John. Now Mr. Wright was a major suspect in the murder of Hans Schneider. But what was André Dumont's involvement in all of this?

"Maybe that's why Mr. Wright was acting so weird when we saw him that day?" asked Elmer. "Maybe the gun he used was under the blanket!"

"Perhaps," said John. "A murder weapon would be helpful if the police had that."

"And then he said he should stop in and see Uncle Ed in case he needed something for his arm…but he never showed up!" Elmer summarized.

"That's right," said John. "And how likely is it that Mr. Wright would forget a potential sale?" John scratched his tight, wavy hair as he thought more.

It was a strange feeling for Summer. On the one hand she felt a ray of hope for her father and his innocence, but on the other hand she felt distressed that it could be a man everyone liked.

"Wait a minute!" said John. "There's a major rally…tomorrow night at the Petrenko's. And Mr. Wright was invited?" John confirmed with his brother.

Elmer nodded, wide-eyed. "That's what Matthew Carver said."

"Then we need to be there," said John simply. "Maybe we can search Mr. Wright's wagon. At the same time, we can see how big this rally gets, because if more than forty or fifty people show up, maybe this area will have another rebellion on its hands, too!"

John figured it was one thing to stand on a wagon and talk passionately to people who were walking by. But holding a big rally was a different kind of message. André Dumont really meant what he said—he was looking to create upheaval. But how was he involved with Earl, who at this point, seemed their best suspect in the murder of Hans Schneider? And what did André mean by delivering a message here and there?

Elmer's eyes were huge with worry and bewilderment. "But how are we going to go? And, how come no one around here has heard of it?" pressed Elmer. "No one's mentioned anything to Father, Mother or Uncle Ed, as far as I know."

John grabbed Elmer by the arm in realization.

"That's just it! They do know!" he said.

"Know what?" said Elmer, retrieving his arm.

"The neighbours, they do know about the rally! Mr. Devonshire was just here this morning and I think he almost told us, but he stopped himself," John explained.

"Why?" asked Summer.

"Because he knows Mother, Father and Uncle Ed would never condone it. They're not exactly the rebellion types, being school teachers, and with Father knowing Sergeant English pretty well…," John continued.

"…then everyone has kept this to themselves!" finished Elmer.

"Yes, and then you add to this the fact that we've been spared the worst of all the problems facing everyone lately, like the fire and the robberies. And we're not exactly the most popular people to recruit for a revolt," said John.

"Summer, what do you think?" prompted John, noticing that she was deep in thought.

"I know something else, I think," she said, alarm in her voice.

"Remember when Mr. Dumont met with Chief Five Hawks? He shook his hand, you said."

"Of course!" exclaimed John, knowing where she was going. "When he saved me at the river, he said something about there being 'change' in the air! You're right, Summer…he's bringing Chief Five Hawks himself to this rally so he can bring the Cree onside!"

"Yes!" agreed Elmer.

"But if the Cree are coming, we have to assume others will be represented there, too," John continued. "The Métis, since Dumont is Métis, and maybe other Indian tribes, too. Not to mention all the homesteaders he's convinced to come."

"But if most people know about this, wouldn't the police?" asked Elmer.

"You'd think so…but they might have their own reasons for not getting involved right now," said John. "Maybe they'll try to stop it before it even begins. Or, maybe not as many people will show up as Mr. Dumont wants."

"This could be the biggest thing that's ever happened here," said Elmer in awe.

"You're right, Elmer," said John seriously. "And tomorrow night, somehow, we need to be there. This might be our last chance to help Summer's father."

***

The next day unfolded slowly. John, Elmer, and Summer worked hard on the homestead, often helping William and Ed with work outside. Sometimes she joined Mary in the kitchen with food preparation.

All of them wondered if somehow one of the adults would learn of the rally. Perhaps a neighbour would come by with news of it, or the Royal North West Mounted Police would burst in with news. But no one came. However, near the day's end, the adults seemed to notice an above average number of wagons going by off in the distance. John's casual mention of hearing some adults in Borden talking about a barn dance tonight at a farm a few miles north of the homestead seemed to be enough to cast away any suspicions.

As evening fell, Summer received permission to sleep in the barn. She told the Diefenbakers she was worried that her horse was not feeling well, and she wanted to be sure Prairie Dancer was alright. William and Mary gave her permission, as long as she slept on the second floor in the hayloft, to be safe from roaming predators, such as the coyotes.

"If Summer's sleeping in the hayloft tonight then Elmer can have the kitchen back. It will give Ed more room," said Mary.

Elmer looked at John with wide eyes and John returned the stare back as if to say, "Say something."

"Um, that's okay, Mother. If it's all the same to you and Father, I'd like to stay at Uncle Ed's, with John," Elmer said. "Summer will likely be back inside the house tomorrow night and then I'd just have to keep changing where I'm sleeping."

Mary stared at her youngest for a moment and then let it go. "Suit yourself, boy."

Farm life tended to make for an early bedtime, and on a day when everyone had worked so hard, John hoped that his uncle would choose one of his earlier bedtimes. Ed didn't disappoint, falling asleep even earlier than they had anticipated. John and Elmer waited for that moment then gingerly stepped outside into the darkened summer evening. Elmer tripped over one of Ed's large boots and almost knocked John over, but they somehow managed to exit without being stopped. They stole toward the barn across the open field where Summer, as planned, had Prairie Dancer, Skipper and Blue ready to ride.

At the barn no one spoke, not even Elmer. Less than five minutes had passed as they led the three horses out of the barn.

As they turned around the corner, all three of them gasped.

"And just where in blazes do you three think you're going?"

The sight of Ed Diefenbaker, now awake, standing in the semi-darkness was almost enough to make John, Elmer, and Summer jump out of their skins. John gulped, knowing that as the eldest he was the one being counted on for answers. John glanced nervously at the main homestead across the field, half expecting his mother to come storming out, too, which he decided would be even worse. However, the homestead was silent as John quickly spoke, spilling everything to his uncle at breakneck speed, other than the fact they strongly suspected Earl of murder. Instead, John focused on the political rally, outlining each time they had met Dumont and what they had talked about. He also told his uncle how he, Elmer, and Summer believe that the rally tonight might spark something larger.

His uncle listened with interest. When John was finished he turned around and looked up at the sky, as if to think without all the distractions. Only the stars and a waning moon stared back at him.

"Wait here," he said simply. Then Ed turned and started to walk towards the main homestead.

"Uncle...Ed?" said John behind him. But his uncle paid no heed to John's confusion.

"Great!" said John sarcastically. "Now he's going to tell Father and Mother. We'll never get to go!"

Elmer and Summer looked dejected. A few nervous minutes passed while John, Elmer, and Summer patted their horses and waited impatiently.

In a few minutes, Ed returned, with William by his side.

The children were certain that they were in deep trouble.

"You know, your father and I both know Sergeant English pretty well," said Ed, as he walked toward them. "It's hard for us to believe he wouldn't be on to this. He's probably shutting it down right now."

"But..." began John nervously.

"And it still doesn't explain to me why you three were about to attend this so-called rally. You're just kids," William interrupted before John could explain.

John felt deflated. Part of him hated still being a kid. Sometimes he got tired of defending himself just because of his age.

"I know it sounds strange, Father, but I think Mr. Dumont really likes me. He always wants to talk politics with me and I just have this feeling that I should be there because it might lead to new information. Something important is going to happen. It's hard to explain." John looked down at the ground.

"Like I said, you're kids," said William. "You're going to need adult supervision."

John looked up again at his father and uncle, his eyes wide. "You mean…"

"Are you going to get these horses hitched up to the wagon or do we have to ride these things bareback?" asked William. "Now let's go."

"Yes sir!" said John and Elmer with glee in their voices while Summer beamed.

"Father?" asked Elmer.

"Yes?"

"Is Mother coming?"

"What do you think, Elmer?"

"I think she's not coming."

"Good guess. Let's just say I'm probably not the most popular man in the world with your mother right now, taking children to a late-night political rally. In fact, if you can move any faster, it would probably be a good thing for all of us."

***

The warm night gave no pause as William, Ed, Elmer, John and Summer pushed toward the Petrenko farm as fast as possible, their thoughts hidden by the deep silence in which they rode. Only the rattle of the wagon broke the night air.

Along the way, William informed John and Elmer that he was not impressed that they had kept so much information to themselves over the past week. On top of that, John had a feeling he and Elmer would have to write essays on these events but he didn't want to ask about it in case he was wrong.

After initial groans, they rode on in silence, through sparse grasses and scattered poplar trees that stuck out of the ground in random clusters. The Northern Lights were out again tonight, something John had not seen since the night Hans Schneider had died. As they scaled a slender knoll, John leaned ahead and saw the familiar dip of the land that led toward the Petrenko farm. Below, a transformation had taken place.

Long flames billowed from makeshift tall candle sticks, their poles held by men anchoring the far-flung corners of the Ukrainian farmer's homestead. The homestead itself was alive with the chatter of what had to be a hundred and fifty voices and scores of horses. John had never seen so many people at once. Although people milled about, talking in small groups and moving from one gathering to another, an empty flatbed wagon was clearly meant to be a stage or platform of some sort. It had been propped up on makeshift supports to give it more height. On either side of the stage were two additional long candles, clearly meant to illuminate this area of the field.

The five travellers slowed their approach now, unloading from the wagon near a cluster of trees. They moved up along the edge of the crowd and found a place to plant themselves.

John could see Mr. Nicolas Petrenko, a tall and husky Ukrainian man, speaking with two other men he didn't recognize.

"Look," Elmer said, pointing to a person standing on a wagon.

André Dumont was unmistakable. It was his confidence that compelled people to lock their eyes on him, allowing his presence to be felt instantly. He wore his trademark sleek and simple black clothing as he stood on the flatbed wagon in front of the crowd.

To André's right was another distinctive personality, the now enigmatic Earl T. Wright. His long, silver moustache and silver hair defined him easily. He stood at the wagon's edge bending down to shake hands and chat with some people in the front row of the crowd.

"Mr. Wright's here," said John quietly to his brother and Summer. "He sure is finding a way to be the centre of attention."

Now Summer bumped John's arm and he looked in the direction that her head was turned. He could see about twenty-five Cree men, dressed in traditional clothing of deer and buffalo skins. Many were wearing beaded vests. They were led with distinction by Chief Five Hawks, who wore a large, ceremonial headdress. Summer, who was unsure how her presence at the rally would be seen from members of her own tribe, tried to stay behind everyone. From over John's shoulder, she also recognized the clothing of the Assiniboine tribe who were long time allies of the Cree. They were there in nearly-equal numbers. All of them wore their traditional clothing, made from animal skins and decorated with beads.

Another group of about twenty were obviously Métis. They were dressed in a combination of elk and deer skins merged with flamboyant stripes of colour sewn into their clothing, a blend of their European and Indian heritage. Many of the men had ornamented thick belts that crossed from front to back across their chests, which carried various pouches. Their eyes were glued to where André and Earl stood.

Everyone else seemed to be homesteaders and business owners from the area. William and Ed obviously recognized a great number of people, given the way they were pointing and talking to each other. Max Taggart, the general store owner was there, as well as the livery stable owner. Only a few wives of homesteaders were in attendance.

Lurking on the edges of the crowd, Elmer spotted the man they knew only as Cecil, the one André had accused of being a whisky smuggler. They watched him talk with a strange man near Cecil's wagon, which was again full of barrels.

As the Diefenbakers and Summer spoke amongst themselves, an old Métis man was slowly riding toward the gathering. He wore a deerskin vest with patterns of bright beads and a colourful red sash that acted as a belt for his pants. The elderly man dismounted from the horse unhurriedly, tying the animal to a tree near the Diefenbaker wagon. The horse looked grateful for the break and began grazing.

John, the only one who had noticed this, nodded respectfully at the Métis elder. He nodded back and quietly sat down on the grass, cross-legged and hunched, a few feet away.

The noise of the crowd gradually quieted. Heads began to turn toward the front with Summer and the Diefenbakers following suit. André Dumont had his hands raised to quiet the remaining murmurs. Earl T. Wright remained beside him, looking out at the crowd and smiling and nodding from person to person.

***

It had been so easy to find him. Wherever there were people, you could always find the double-crossing lowlife. What a glory hound! After hitching a ride on a wagon north of Borden, all he had to do was listen carefully in on conversations to find out about this rally. Now, as an audience member in the middle of the crowd, he would simply stay quiet until he could make his way to the front and seize his moment. He should have stolen a gun first. No problem. The knife strapped to his leg would do just as well. He would take care of him soon, in front of all these people. Sure, he would be caught and probably never see the light of day again, but it would be worth it. He would expose him, eliminate him. It would be worth it to see his prey suffer, as he had suffered himself. It would be worth it to show him that one cannot escape the past.

***

"My friends, you will remember this night," André projected in his usual confident voice.

He instantly had their attention.

"This is the night when we begin to truly build a voice that the government must hear. I want to especially welcome Chief Five Hawks of the Cree and Chief Fallen Branch of the Assiniboine. I have been to your communities and I have felt your pain. I have felt your need to create a new deal for your people.

"From the Métis, from my own people, let me welcome Chief Bergeron and many of his band who hail from Bellevue, northeast of here. My uncle would have been proud to see so many of you here together, united in this great cause."

The spontaneous applause from a few people in the crowd

delayed André for a moment.

During this pause, John looked quizzical. "Father, Mr. Dumont didn't mention Batoche. Why isn't anyone here from the Batoche-area Métis? Wouldn't it make sense for Mr. Dumont to bring people from the village where his uncle once lived?"

William considered John's words. "It does seem odd," he replied.

Just as André was about to speak again, he was interrupted by a loud clearing of the throat beside him. André glanced over to see Earl had nudged closer, raising his silver eyebrows at André, as if to remind him of something.

"Yes, very well," said André, without his usual enthusiasm. "Mr. Earl T. Wright, the Rawleigh's man, would like me to remind you that he will be available afterwards for all your purchasing needs."

Another loud clearing of the throat. Earl smiled at André.

"Yes," said André impatiently. "Ten percent off for the first forty sales he makes tonight."

Then André glared at Earl to make him back off from trying to be the centre of the show.

William put his hand on John's shoulder. "Ed and I are going over to talk with Max Taggart. We'll be right back. You three don't go far."

John nodded as André continued his speech. The old Métis man on the grass kept looking at John and then looking back at the stage. John ignored him for the moment then quickly spun toward Elmer.

"Why don't you and Summer find Mr. Wright's wagon and see if you can locate the murder weapon?" John said.

"But…I don't know where the wagon is!" said Elmer nervously.

"Elmer, it's canary yellow, for Pete's sake!" said John. "And it was your idea that maybe that's what he was hiding!"

"Well, what are *you* going to do?" wondered Elmer.

"I'm going to speak with that elderly Métis man over there," John said, nodding his head towards him.

"He keeps looking at me so maybe I can find something out."

"Okay. I can see his wagon now. We'll be back soon!"

Elmer and Summer left, making sure William and Ed were not looking their way.

André had resumed speaking, now that he had gotten Earl to back off a bit, and was in full swing again.

"…better to be here, my friends, under the cover of darkness, than meet in these large numbers by the light of day," spoke André with his eyes on fire. "It is our lot, for now, to have a cause that exists in the shadows. But very soon we will be a force, a force large enough to speak to the federal government so that they will finally listen!"

A cheer went up from the crowd.

"Soon, I promise you, we will take our concerns to the streets of our towns and our countryside in the full light of day. We will take back the West from a government who doesn't care about the people. We will take back what is ours…with force, if necessary!"

Chapter 15

The Fallen

Another cheer went up from the crowd. John had spent a few minutes with the Métis elder and then walked back to the place where he had been standing before. He waved to his father who was craning his neck to see if John was alright.

A few moments later, Summer and Elmer came running back breathlessly. Elmer began shaking his head while he caught his breath.

"The only things we found under Mr. Wright's blanket were some tools, a basket of Saskatoon berries and a bunch of encyclopedias," said Elmer. "I think those were the things that were sticking out of the blanket that day."

John looked perplexed. "I don't get it. Why would he want to hide something like that?"

The force of André's words—passionate and forceful—made them turn toward the front to listen.

"Laurier glosses over problems and opens the floodgates to everyone in the West and then satisfies no one."

"Here, here!" shouted several men.

John thought about the rebellion stories Sergeant English had told only a week ago. Had it really only been a week? He wondered if history was about to repeat itself.

"The Métis have been pushed further away or intruded upon. The government says it knows best when the Métis, Cree and Assiniboine no longer wander wherever they please to follow the hunt…"

A roar of approval went up from the Métis and Indians.

"…and the Cree and Assiniboine are forced to live where the government says to live…!"

The Indians were shouting their approval from the crowd, creating a buzz of excitement.

André felt a surge of conviction.

"And for you white settlers…your government says it knows best while farmers can't find a fair price for their wheat. You have come looking for a dream and all you have found is hardship."

His voice cracked with emotion as he continued.

"The government says it knows best when it takes children from their homes," André spoke with bitterness, "and places them with people who don't love them and don't look out for them."

Many people clapped, even though they weren't sure what André was getting at now.

"The government says it knows best," said André, "but it knows nothing of fairness and nothing of compassion. Children need guidance, they need..." his voice cracked and trailed off as if he didn't know where he was going with his sentence, either.

There was another smattering of applause before someone shouted something unexpected.

"The government's not going to listen to murderers!"

André stopped and looked toward the speaker in the middle of the crowd. It seemed to snap him out of his haze.

"Who said that? What do you mean?" André asked.

"Michael Hewson," the man shouted, identifying himself. "Why should the government listen to us if we partner with the Cree? It was a Cree who murdered Hans Schneider!"

A cascade of murmurs interrupted and John, Elmer, and Summer craned their necks to see what was going on. Try as they might, they couldn't get a good view.

Just then, Chief Five Hawk's bellowed. "River's Voice did not murder anyone!"

"Well, he's the one sitting in prison right now, and I say let him rot," shouted the same settler.

"He is in prison because the police made a mistake. What about the pelts stolen from our reservation?" the Chief challenged. "The Cree have had many things taken from them in the last week."

"Yeah, well, you're not the only ones!" someone shouted.

"Almost everyone I know has had something taken. How do we know this isn't Indian-doing, taking revenge because one of your own is in jail?"

Now Chief Fallen Branch joined in the heated debate. "You think all Indians are the same? Why do you say 'Indian-doing'? We are Assiniboine. We are not the Cree."

Chief Bergeron of the Métis now made his voice heard. "You settlers are all the same. You walk around this land as if it has always been yours and you blame others for problems you make yourselves."

"I'll show you what a problem looks like," another settler shouted. Soon about a dozen men were fighting with one another, some arguing, others pushing and shoving. It was on the verge of turning into a full-scale riot and André Dumont suddenly, shockingly, looked completely out of control. Earl had shrunk back some on the wagon, sensing things were starting to take a turn for the worse. If there was one thing Earl T. Wright knew how to gauge it was when a good deal was going wrong.

"Friends, we must not…" André began. Something whizzed by his head and just missed him as the crowd began to argue and push each other more.

"Look here!" he hollered. But no one was listening.

John could feel an adrenalin rush and felt compelled to act on it.

"I'm going up there, stay here."

"John, you just can't just leave. You're not allowed to go up there," Elmer said desperately. He didn't know what had gotten into his normally shy brother. Now all of a sudden he wanted to talk to one hundred and fifty people—people who were definitely not in a good mood right now. Elmer looked toward their father and uncle but they hadn't yet noticed John's intent. He had never seen his brother's eyes look so intense.

John sprang from his place on the edge of the crowd and moved with great speed toward the front of the large group, darting in and out until he reached the front, while the old Métis man's eyes followed him carefully. John made a flying leap for the wagon and landed on his feet right beside André.

***

What's this? Another distraction? Surely this boy will not be on the stage for long. The man stayed in the middle of the audience, although he continued to move slowly toward the front, a half shuffle at a time. Then he would not waste any more time, blending in like this. Boy or no boy, he was going to make his move.

***

Andre staggered backwards, looking startled.

"John Diefenbaker?"

John ignored him and looked out at the crowd.

"Just look at you!" shouted John.

The crowd turned as one in surprise at the young-sounding voice. Some men still held the front of one another's shirts, the fabric clenched up in their fists. William and Ed, standing beside Max Taggart, wondered how 'Don't go far' somehow meant to go jump up on the stage.

"My name is John Diefenbaker. It seems very strange to me that we're fighting with each other," his voice rang out. "Out here, we're used to helping each other, aren't we?"

A few people slowly nodded their heads.

"Helping each other is how we've made the West what it is. My father, mother, and uncle…they always tell my brother and me that we have to contribute if we're going to make it. It's the only way. Otherwise we may as well just give up right now."

Everyone stared at John, actually waiting for his next few words. John sensed this and caught his breath; he felt like he could do anything for the briefest of moments.

"Some of you know I'm the one who found Mr. Schneider a few moments after he was killed. Now I don't know who actually did it. I thought I knew, but now I'm not sure. But I know who didn't do it. River's Voice has been a family friend for years and his daughter is like a sister to my brother and me. We don't have the truth yet, but I know it will come soon."

John looked out at the old Métis man and toward his brother and Summer. No one said anything, so he kept going. His father and uncle were dumbstruck with pride and apprehension.

"We all have differences between us, whether it's the language we speak, the shade of our skin, or the sound of our name. I'm just an average Canadian, but you know what? I'm different, too. My last name is German because my grandfather happened to come from Germany. But I'm free, that's what my father always reminds us. As I grow up in this country, I know I'm free to speak without fear or to stand up for what I think is right. We can choose who we want to run our country and we once chose a man named Sir John A. Macdonald..."

Cheers at the sound of Macdonald's name began to ripple in a cascade of spontaneous pride but John kept going, fueled by their enthusiasm. He put one hand on his hip and wagged his finger at the audience as if he were about to scold someone.

"...and Sir John gave his life to this country! He built the railway that linked Canada from ocean to ocean and if Sir John opened the doors of the West, then Prime Minister Laurier has sent everyone through those doors and filled the West...with us!"

William bit his lip hard to stop the surge of emotions he was feeling.

"Here, here!" many shouted.

"The boy's right," another voice rang out.

"That's my nephew!" Ed told a few strangers proudly.

Even Earl, who was still on the wagon platform behind André and John, seemed stirred by John's speaking.

***

Why won't this boy just leave the stage, he wondered impatiently. He wasn't going to wait any longer. Enough is enough. The man began to move toward the stage, ever closer.

***

John continued. "If things feel uncertain now, maybe it's only because we're being told they are…by him," he said, gesturing toward André. The young Métis man looked uncomfortable, but didn't move. Earl began to nod, always eager to demonstrate he was on the winning team.

"We must not turn against one another," John continued. "In fact, we must not listen to this man!" John said, now pointing directly at André. "He's not even who he says he is! He is not the nephew of Gabriel Dumont. I know this because a Métis elder just told me so."

Murmurs of confusion went up from the crowd.

***

Closer, closer now. He needed to be in the front row to reach him, to make his move. He pulled his hat down lower over his eyes.

***

André looked shocked at John's words and then a forced grin grew on his face. Earl, too, looked surprised. All three of them on the wagon seemed unsure of what to do next. Then André tried to diffuse the situation.

"Thank you for your heartfelt speech, young John. But go home now, lad. Of course I am who I say I am. I am indeed Gabriel Dumont's nephew."

At this point Earl reached over and placed his hand on André's shoulder and asked him a question that John could not hear.

***

"Now!"

The man from the audience sprang forward, propelling himself from a wooden block that had been set up beside the stage. He knocked André Dumont across the wagon, the flash of a long metal knife visible under the muted light of the tall, lit candlesticks. John, who had seen someone lunging out of the corner of his eye, had already leapt off the stage and rolled to safety on the ground. A shocked Earl fell off the end of the wagon by accident in his haste to retreat, landing on his back and knocking the wind out of himself.

The crowd gasped and William and Ed yelled "John!" at the same time, as they pushed their way toward the front of the crowd. John looked over his shoulder and saw André and the stranger wrestling for control of the knife. William and Ed grabbed John and whisked him back to the edge of the crowd, where Elmer and Summer quickly joined them. Close on their heels was Earl, who ran like a rabbit despite his age.

Several men in the crowd had stepped forward, trying to see if they could help in some way, but the threat of the swinging blade, which so far André had managed to avoid, made it difficult for them to intervene.

"You thought you could get away with it, didn't you?" said the stranger venomously. He had managed to pin André on his back, the stranger's hat now off. André looked shocked at seeing the scarred face of the stranger, but he managed to grab his attacker's wrists and was so far preventing him from using the knife. As the attacker pushed with extra pressure, the blade bearing down now on André's neck, the sound of three loud gunshots splintered the night air.

Everyone turned their heads to see twelve Royal North West Mounted Police officers burst onto the field on horseback, their trademark bright red uniforms unmistakable. They were led by Sergeant English and Constable Wood. A thirteenth officer brought up the rear with a horse and wagon.

The stranger instantly scrambled away from André, his knife still in hand. He ran in the opposite direction of the dozen mounted police officers. Sergeant English nodded to Constable Wood, giving him permission to apprehend the fleeing man.

"Cyrus Ramsey! Stop!" Constable Wood hollered. But Cyrus had no intention of stopping, or even slowing down. Constable Wood squeezed his horse's sides with his heels and accelerated.

Constable Wood's horse galloped after and quickly overtook the fleeing man. The officer drew his horse beside the knife-wielding man and leapt, landing on top of him. He knocked Cyrus to the ground watching him roll two feet away, the knife landing beside him. The fugitive reached for the knife, whirling around to face the officer. By this time, Constable Wood had already drawn his gun, pointing it directly at the snarling face before him.

"I'm only going to ask you this once," said Constable Wood. "Drop it."

***

Meanwhile, as the police burst onto the scene, the grizzled, limping Cecil had jumped into his wagon as fast as he could,

203

immediately ending his deal with someone in the crowd. One of the police officers quickly intercepted him, steering his horse directly in front of the rickety wagon filled with barrels.

As Cecil was protesting the seizure of his wagon, Sergeant English joined the other officers momentarily to oversee.

"It's water, just plain water. I don't even drink!" Cecil protested.

One of the officers popped open a spout near the top of the barrel and tipped it into his cupped hand, tasting it. He frowned in confusion.

"It is water, Sergeant. He's right. No whisky here."

Sergeant English scowled.

"We'll see about that. Step back," he said in his deep voice. He pulled out his gun and shot the barrel near the bottom. Liquid came gushing out and he pointed to the same officer.

"No!" howled Cecil.

"Now taste it."

The officer cupped his hand and took a sip.

"Whisky! How…?" the officer began.

The sergeant knocked on the top of one of the barrels. "False top. He keeps a few inches of water in the top and all the rest is whisky. Got a tip last week there were a few American smugglers getting a bit more creative in their whisky sales. Arrest him. He's the least of my worries. I've got an escaped murderer to deal with. And a would-be rebellion leader."

Moments later, Sergeant English climbed up to the centre of the makeshift stage with the intent of clearing out the shocked crowd. Three quarters of the crowd hadn't moved as they tried to figure out what was going on. The rest had fled, once the officers had arrived, not wanting to be involved in any way.

A subdued André stood surrounded by numerous police officers, clearly in their custody as well. He and Cyrus Ramsey, who was also secured by several burly police officers, glared at one another.

"This meeting is now over," Sergeant English projected in his deep voice.

Someone from the audience spoke up. "Chester Atkinson, I'm a reporter from the *Langham Times*. Who is that man?" he asked, pointing to André. "The Diefenbaker boy said he's not related to Gabriel Dumont at all."

Sergeant English glowered at the reporter but decided to answer. It wouldn't do any harm to be in the papers, especially for a success like this, the sergeant realized. He figured it would be good publicity for people to know that the Mounties always get their man.

"The Diefenbaker boy was right," said Sergeant English. "This man is no relation to the rebel leader. In fact, his real name is André Dupont, not Dumont."

The crowd gasped. John, standing at the front of the audience with his father, uncle, Elmer, and Summer was still astonished, even though the Métis elder had assured him he was no relation to the rebel leader. André had seemed so passionate about this cause. Why would he pretend to be someone he was not? The crowd began chattering until the sergeant began speaking again.

"Dupont and this man, Cyrus Ramsey," he said, gesturing to the scar-faced man, "were partners in a few bank heists in Winnipeg. Although Dupont was out of his league when he got mixed up with this one.

"Ramsey is a convicted murderer. He killed three people in cold blood two years ago and he was sentenced to life in prison. We learned that even his Winnipeg lawyer didn't want to represent him anymore. He said it would go against his principles."

"Wow, a lawyer with integrity. Who was it?" asked the reporter.

"Let's see…an Arthur Meighen," the sergeant replied after checking his notepad.

"Never heard of him," said the reporter to himself.

The sergeant continued. "But Cyrus Ramsey managed to escape even before arriving at the prison. A few months ago, he and Dupont made the unfortunate choice of teaming up to rob a bank in Winnipeg. Police arrived in time to capture Ramsey. Dupont however, escaped."

"Abandoned me more like it!" shouted Ramsey from where he stood surrounded by officers. "I was left to rot and there was no way I was going to allow some smooth-talking, two-faced liar get away with it!"

"It's not my fault you weren't fast enough to escape," Andre fired back. "I didn't turn you in, you made your own bed."

Ramsey began struggling more. The police forced him further away from André and away from the crowd, too.

The reporter was writing furiously. "So the train escape the other night...that was Ramsey?" he asked.

The sergeant nodded. "Yes. He escaped while being transferred to another prison because of overcrowding. He learned that Dupont was in the Borden area and timed his escape for that stop. This time, he'll be personally escorted wherever he goes until the courts can put him away for good."

Chester fired off another question. "Then Dupont changed his name to Dumont and adopted a Métis identity?"

"Oh, he really is Métis, but an urban Métis from Winnipeg, Manitoba. With Dupont's last name being similar, we think he began to fantasize about being related to the real Dumont and researched his life to be convincing. His parents were poor, trying to make a life in Winnipeg. Unfortunately, his father died when Dupont was very young and his mother abandoned him when he was just twelve. Rough time, right before a boy becomes a man."

"You lie! My mother loved me! She wouldn't do that... she... couldn't have done..." André began.

The sergeant went on. "When a representative of the govern-ment heard about the boy living alone, he found Dupont at home with another family in Winnipeg who agreed to adopt him. I think they made a mistake there. According to the information we gathered, he was regularly mistreated. And that's when he began getting into trouble with the law, mainly through lying and cheating, just enough to get by."

"My mother loves me," repeated André, almost in a hoarse whisper. "It was the government that took my life away. The government worker ruined everything, don't you see? They took me away and gave me to others...people who didn't want me..."

John stared at the slumped shoulders of the young man who had seemed so confident, so sure of himself only a short time ago. Andre had mobilized so many people in such a short period of time, inspiring them with his words. He had inter-vened to help John, Elmer, and Summer from the shady whisky smuggler in Borden and had saved John from drowning in the North Saskatchewan River. He had challenged everything John believed about life in the West. Now, he seemed very different in these last few minutes. The truth had transformed him into another person, a smaller man who was weighed down with great sadness.

The crowd was now near frenzy because of the information overload. Sergeant English decided to take the opportunity to acknowledge how much had happened in the past week.

"Look, folks, it's been a busy week for a small town. We've had a homesteader tragically killed, a con artist here take up much of our time, thefts, a prairie fire and a prisoner escape. We have reinforcements now from Saskatoon and we're going to get to the bottom of all of these things."

Summer looked at John in confusion, and John realized the saying confused her. "Getting to the bottom of these things means they're going to figure out what happened," explained John. As he explained this, John felt his stomach flip. He took a step forward from the crowd toward Sergeant English.

"Sergeant English?" said John, projecting his voice well.

"Yes, hello young Diefenbaker!" said the sergeant in a good natured way, causing the crowd to laugh.

"Sergeant, with all due respect, you haven't found the killer of Mr. Hans Schneider yet."

The crowd immediately gave a combination of gasps and instant chattering until the sergeant held up his hand for quiet.

He peered at John intently.

"Son, I know River's Voice is a friend of your family's, but..."

"Sergeant English, I can prove it," interrupted John.

Chapter 16

Going Home

Sergeant English attempted to dismiss whatever John was about to say, but the crowd would have none of it, including the reporter. They still remembered the image of John standing tall and inspiring with his words just moments before.

"Let's hear what the boy has to say!" shouted a settler.

"Yes, we want to hear!" shouted members of the Cree.

"Fine," said the sergeant, half amused. "What do you have, son?"

John took a deep breath while his family looked on.

"A great deal of your case is based upon the eyewitness account of Mr. and Mrs. Jennings, who said they saw River's Voice and Mr. Schneider arguing. The Jennings apparently heard River's Voice threaten Mr. Schneider. One day later, Mr. Schneider was murdered.

"That's right," said Sergeant English. "Eyewitnesses are always important in police work."

"Except in this case," said John, "your eyewitnesses claim

they heard River's Voice threaten Mr. Schneider with 'You'll pay for this.'"

"Yes, what of it?" asked Sergeant English.

"With all due respect to River's Voice, English is a language he still finds very challenging. Even his daughter, my friend Summer Storm here," John said, gesturing to Summer, "has had more English language instruction, and she doesn't yet recognize common English sayings. I would suggest there is no way the Jennings heard River's Voice say 'You'll pay for this.' He would not even have known what that meant."

Talking instantly rippled across the crowd. Sergeant English began to entrench his position.

"We still have his necklace that was found on the Schneider's property."

"Yes," said John, "but we know that River's Voice visited the Schneider farm once before and he believes he may have lost it then."

"Son, why are you so determined to complicate things?" The senior police officer felt pressure to try and preserve the arrest he had originally made.

"I'm sorry, Sergeant, that is not my intention. But I visited River's Voice in prison last week…"

"You did what?" he asked, perturbed.

"…and I know I shouldn't have been there," added John. "I told him I'd leave no stone unturned in finding out the truth."

John paused for dramatic effect. "By the way, he didn't know what that meant either, but I just wanted to keep my promise."

The crowd erupted into loud chatter. The Cree felt a collective surge of hope. William placed his hand on John's shoulder and squeezed it, letting his eldest son know that he supported him.

"Young Diefenbaker is right again!" someone shouted.

"Listen to the boy!" another voice from the back could be heard.

As Sergeant English tried to quell the noise by holding up his arms, a sheepish-looking man and woman moved toward Constable Wood from where they had been standing in the crowd. John recognized them as Kyle and Isabelle Jennings—the police eyewitnesses! They had been at the rally all this time.

The tall constable bent his ear toward them, nodding a few times and then all the colour seemed to drain from his face. The athletic officer hopped onto the stage and apparently repeated something in a low voice to Sergeant English. The sergeant, too, looked dismayed. He cleared his throat. Certainly, he could shut down the meeting down right now, but at this point the veteran police officer would risk causing a riot, especially with the Cree and Assiniboine here in such large numbers.

"Upon further reflection," began Sergeant English, "Mr. and Mrs. Jennings say they may have made an error in what they heard that day. It seems that the enthusiasm for being a part of the excitement of an arrest led them to state that they heard River's Voice utter a death threat."

The crowd held its breath. Indians and Métis alike wanted to know that one of their own was innocent. And the non-Native people loved the idea of one of their own, especially just a boy, showing up the police force.

"In fact, they now say they were too far away to hear anything."

The Cree, the Assiniboine, the Métis, and even many of the settlers erupted into a cheer.

"Free River's Voice!" shouted Chief Five Hawks.

"Free him! He is innocent!" others yelled.

Summer felt her stomach flip.

John was amazed that the crowd was so much on River's Voice's side now but was so against him earlier. He began to realize that people sometimes think differently when they are in groups. He looked over at Earl and seemed torn whether or not to speak out about his strange behavior, too. But something wasn't quite right. John was still missing something and his instincts told him to wait.

Sergeant English scowled before responding.

"River's Voice told us himself that he believed Hans Schneider stole a large collection of his pelts. That's motive for the crime. And we have no other credible suspect."

John suddenly had the realization he was looking for. "Fox

and beaver pelts, right Sergeant? Found in the Schneider's barn?"

The sergeant looked surprised. "Yes…but how did you know that? We haven't released that information yet. I asked Gertrude not to mention what kinds of pelts were found nor where they were found because it was part of our ongoing investigation."

"Mrs. Schneider didn't tell me, Sergeant. So you might want to ask Mr. Dupont that question. He's the one who told me what kind of pelts and where they were found. He told me this when we saw him near the Long River Reservation, along the banks of the North Saskatchewan River. So the question is how did *he* know?"

The crowd began to buzz again.

"In some way, Sergeant," said John, speaking over the increasing crowd noises, "Mr. Dupont is involved in all of this. And perhaps it has something to do with the murder of Hans Schneider after all."

"The man has an alibi. He was in the hotel the night of the murder," began Sergeant English.

"Yes, but what if he wasn't working alone?" surmised John. "What if someone else was in that field when Mr. Schneider died?"

Sergeant English was regretting that he had tried to do any of this publicly for the sake of a good newspaper story. The reporter, Chester, was writing furiously now. Before the sergeant could reply, a quiet voice spoke up from behind the stage, just barely audible.

"Duncan took them."

It was André.

"I beg your pardon?" asked Sergeant English, turning towards his prisoner. The officers who held him brought him forward more so he could be heard more clearly.

"John Diefenbaker is right. Duncan Rainey, a man I work with, took the pelts," André said more clearly. "His job was to take things from the Indians and Métis and place them on the property of white settlers and then to do the same in reverse. One of those things was a Cree-made necklace he had found on the reservation.

"The necklace!" said John.

Andre continued. "When he found, and then stole, a valuable collection of pelts from the Cree man's shed, I asked him to plant those in the Schneider's barn."

"Why?" asked Constable Wood.

"I had heard Hans Schneider was prejudiced against all Indians and I knew this would help to build up conflicts and disagreements between Indians and white settlers."

The crowd gasped.

"I asked him to use the necklace he had also taken and plant it in the field of Hans Schneider. That's when he went to drop the necklace in the field, but he…he found…"

"He found Mr. Schneider working in the field late that night and was caught in the act. So he killed him," said John, "rather than be captured."

André nodded.

A surge of voices from the crowd ensued and the remaining police officers moved forward to prevent them from coming closer to the front where André was in custody.

"No one was supposed to get hurt," said André sadly and quietly all of a sudden, speaking only to John now. "I was very angry when he told me he had killed someone. I also told him to leave your family's homestead alone, John. I told him to spare the Diefenbaker's or he would answer to me."

John stared into André's eyes as William and Ed looked at one another in astonishment. That explained why nothing bad had happened on their own homestead, other than the near-miss by the fire caused by the storm. The officers worked to contain the crowd again.

Sergeant English shook his head in disbelief at the turn of events.

"It seems as if we have a budding lawyer in our midst," he said, looking directly at John and speaking over the noise.

"At our earliest opportunity tomorrow morning…and given this new information…" the sergeant began, after a pause.

The crowd noise abruptly stopped as everyone held their breath.

"River's Voice will be free to go home."

Cheers erupted across the field, and no one shouted with more joy than the Cree and no one among the Cree more than Summer Storm. John blushed as his father, uncle, Elmer, and Summer slapped him on the back and hugged him. Many of the Cree came forward to thank John. Chief Five Hawks nodded to John in silence, with just a hint of amusement playing about his face. The Métis, too, were pleased that André would no longer be impersonating the nephew of Gabriel Dumont, for the real Dumont was revered for his exploits across the prairies.

Sergeant English jumped off the wagon to speak with André and two other officers. Immediately afterwards, a few other officers set about dispersing the remainder of the crowd. John inched closer and heard Sergeant English issue new orders.

"Tessier, I want you and Howe to find Mr. Duncan Rainey who is apparently camped out on the northwest corner of the old Stinson farm, a few miles from here. Ask William or Ed Diefenbaker for more detailed directions," said the sergeant, motioning the two men over to their group. William and Ed proceeded to share their knowledge of the area with the officers who were from out of town. Within a short time, the two officers leapt onto their horses and sped away, leaving small eddies of dust swirling on the ground behind their fast-moving steeds.

Summer, surrounded by the Cree now, began to cry in relief as she struggled to absorb everything. Her father had not committed the crime he was accused of. She had always known this, and now, thankfully, everyone else did, too. A few Cree neighbours put their arms around her shoulders, giving her quick hugs. She felt exhilarated with what this meant—her father would soon be home where he belonged.

While Summer talked with members of the Cree, John and Elmer looked over at Earl, who was uncharacteristically keeping to himself. Before John had a chance to say hello, Earl moved briskly to his trademark canary yellow wagon, looking over his shoulder once. He climbed aboard his wagon, pulled his hat on tighter and commanded his two horses to leave the area at a brisk trot.

John wondered about his quick exit but his eyes were drawn to someone else right now. As the noise level continued unabated, John couldn't help but notice André, who stood sullenly between two officers with his arms secured behind his back, looking small, frail and alone. He was a shell of the man John had observed before, looking worn out and very confused. André seemed to be in a different place now, a different time, even. John felt uncomfortable watching him when he realized the officers were taking him to their wagon.

As he was being led away, André suddenly turned to John.

"Have you seen my mother, John? I think she's at home, don't you?"

John didn't know what to say, so he nodded quietly. It didn't seem right to argue with him when something this painful had changed him, something that had triggered his mind to deny the truth so deeply.

"We're going to get him some help," said Sergeant English kindly to John, showing more compassion than John had expected. "He may even be sent to his home city of Winnipeg."

As André was led closer to the wagon, he continued to talk to John.

"Did you hear that, John? I'm going home. We're lucky to have such loving parents, aren't we, John? You and I will do great things some day. Great things."

He looked serene as he climbed into the wagon, believing with all his heart that he was going home.

Chapter 17

The Chief

Mesmerizing wheat fields danced promisingly in the cool prairie morning as the Diefenbaker Schooner made its way to Borden. Everything seemed especially quiet after so much up-heaval. The night before had left few people unaffected.

William and Mary were up front, talking quietly, while Ed, John and Elmer were squeezed into the back. Summer was not with them. She had gone home with relatives after the rally, in time for her father's triumphant return the next morning. The Cree had let William know that they would retrieve her things, including her horse, in a day or two.

John and Elmer were exhausted but it wasn't as if they were allowed to sleep in. In fact, if the police had not asked William and Ed to make a statement at the station today and to bring John and Elmer with him, they knew they would likely be working double-time for Mary Diefenbaker, after all that had happened.

However, if Mary was still angry that William had allowed

the boys to attend the rally, she did not show it. It probably had a lot to do with the outcome—the establishment of the innocence of River's Voice, the capture of several criminals, and, perhaps, the prevention of a full-scale rebellion.

As for John, he was still basking in his father's praise from the ride home last night. He played it over in his mind.

"I'm very proud of you, John. The way you were able to hold the crowd with the conviction of your words and your insistence on finding out the truth. We're going to support your education when the time comes, no doubt about it. Good work, son."

Once at the police station, it only took about twenty minutes for the Diefenbakers to make their official statements.

"When was River's Voice let go?" asked John.

"We released him at dawn," the sergeant replied. "We offered him a ride but he wouldn't hear of it. He said he just wanted to walk the fields and watch the sun rise on his way home. We apologized for the time he spent in here and all he did was shake our hands and smile. We watched him walk down the steps and then he turned west toward the reservation, singing the entire way."

Everyone looked happy with the description of River Voice's release from prison.

"Were your men able to catch that Duncan Rainey fellow, the one Dupont said actually killed Hans?" asked Ed.

Sergeant English snorted as if there was a good story behind his answer.

"Oh, we got him alright. But not without a chase. My men pursued him all the way to Borden. He had himself a good horse, that's for sure. When he got to Borden the late train was there. It had stopped for a few minutes before it went on through, but it was about to leave. So then he gets an idea into his head how to escape my officers."

"What kind of idea?" asked John.

"He thought he'd get off his horse and jump into a train car that he saw was open on both sides. He planned on closing the doors once he jumped off onto the other side. That way he could make his escape with the long train blocking my officers."

"But it didn't work?" asked Elmer.

"Well, it probably would have but he didn't count on what happened next. As he shut the first door on my officers who were getting closer, he turned to jump out the other side. But the other door was slammed in his face and then locked from the outside. Thing is, some young kid who was working on the train at the time…"

The sergeant paused as he checked his notes.

"…a Matthew Carver, saw the man being chased down by the officers. So when Rainey entered the train and shut the first door, the kid locked the other side and trapped him in there until my men caught up. Can you imagine?"

"Matthew!" yelled Elmer. He explained to everyone how he and Summer had met Matthew Carver.

"Well, good thing for us that he found employment on the railway then," Sergeant English said with a smile.

Before the Diefenbakers left the station, Sergeant English thanked everyone for their assistance in the case, singling out John for the way he had taken control of the crowd before the police had a chance to arrive.

"From what I heard, you may have been the difference between a riot and the outcome we ended up with," said the sergeant.

"I think Mr. Dupont meant for everyone's anger to be channeled against the government, not to turn against one another. His dream was to be a famous rebellion leader like Gabriel Dumont, his hero. But he wasn't able to contain all of the passions people felt on all sides," John reflected. "He didn't know what to do once he unleashed it all, kind of like the story of Pandora's box from Greek mythology, right, Father?"

William nodded. "It's a good analogy, son. When people start pointing fingers at one another, a lot of undesirable traits can come out, that's for sure."

Sergeant English shook his head. "Stealing things from some people and leaving them in one another's property as a strategy to create distrust and chaos. Who would have thought of that?"

As the Diefenbakers left the police station, John spotted Earl T. Wright's carriage in front of the printing shop. The main street of Borden, dirt brown and dusty, allowed his canary yellow wagon to stick out easily. Seeing the Diefenbakers approaching, he tipped his wide-brimmed hat toward them.

"Howdy, William, Mary, Ed," said Earl, as they jumped out. "Howdy all," he added, seeing John and Elmer.

"You disappeared on us last night," Ed said. It was obvious that everyone, other than Mary who hadn't been there, was wondering why Earl had been on stage with André in the first place. John had a feeling the police were wondering as well.

"No, no, I left once all the action started," said Earl. "This old heart can't take that kind of excitement anymore," he said, his silver hair peeking out from behind his hat onto his shoulders.

Ed nodded, unconvinced.

William picked up on this theme.

"Well, I have to say, Earl, the boys actually thought you might have been involved in something suspicious."

Earl glanced up with a peculiar expression. "Suspicious? Me? Now why would you think that?" he asked, although he somehow managed to look the part, at least a little.

John cleared his throat. "Well, with all due respect, Mr. Wright, it was for a couple of reasons, sir. First, after the fire when we saw you go by that day, you were trying to hide something in your wagon from us. You even told us it was blankets when we could see it was a collection of various things. You also said you were going to stop in at the house to see if Uncle Ed needed anything for his arm, but you never did."

Earl didn't say anything, so John took this as an invitation to continue.

"The next day," John continued, "Elmer and Summer were in Langham with Uncle Ed. They saw you shake hands with Mr. Dupont. As well, Elmer and Summer overheard you say: 'I liked Hans, but, as I said, he surprised me. But enough about that. What do you need from me if I agree to this?'"

Earl looked both pale and fascinated as John painted his understanding of the last few days' events.

"Only one day later, you were here at the rally created by Mr. Dumont, er, Dupont. Right up on the wagon with him, in fact."

"Now hold on, hold on," said Earl with his hands up in the air defensively. "Now what you saw in the wagon was just an old salesman trying to make a living." He sighed and looked around. "And I expect you'll all keep this information to yourselves, you hear?" Everyone nodded, unsure of what he was going to say.

"A man has a reputation to uphold," Earl added for good measure.

"For your information, under the blanket were some tools, a bucket of Saskatoon berries and a Ridpath encyclopedia set, or at least thirteen out of fifteen volumes anyway. The set's broken."

"That's what I saw last night at the rally!" said Elmer. "Oops!" he added, realizing he had just given away the fact that he and Summer had snooped in Earl's carriage during the rally.

Mary didn't look impressed.

"You boys really get around don't you?" said Earl.

"Well…why were you trying to hide those things?" asked Elmer, feeling embarrassed.

"Because I took them in trade for some tonics, kitchen spices and salves from various customers. But I can't make a living if everyone thinks they can just pawn their stuff off on old Earl T. all the time! I just can't earn a living that way if everyone thinks they can trade with me," he said.

"Then, why did you do it?" asked John.

"Because I was feeling kind of sorry for the Turner's and the Wentzell's. They got hit by the fire, too, and I was trying to do them a good turn, that's all. Then, I got to thinking so much about those trades and what that would do to my business if folks found out I was open to trades and then told others…well, I just got lost in thought and plumb forgot to stop in to see you Ed, and for that I'm sorry."

"I understand," said Ed.

"Well, that was sure nice of you to help the other families," said John. "You gave up your profit on those sales."

"It's nothing," said Earl sniffing.

"But what about seeing you in Langham with Mr. Dupont?"

began Elmer.

"And," added John, "the fact that you said Mr. Schneider surprised you. Well, for a while we thought you meant in the field, you know, on the night of the murder."

Earl burst out in laughter. His face revealed that he felt a combination of amusement and disbelief at the accusation.

"Old Earl T.? Kill someone? You must be joking! I was talking about the fact that I was surprised old Hans could work that late at his age! We were just talking about current events, that's all."

John was glad he realized in time that André Dupont was more of a suspect than Earl. It could have been very embarrassing if they had gone to the police first.

"Then just what were you talking to Dupont about in Langham?" asked Ed.

"Well, that André fellow approached me with two things. First, he had a cut on his arm. Said he did it saving someone from drowning, which I highly doubted. You have to get up pretty early to fool old Earl T."

John and Elmer looked at each other and tried to keep a straight face.

"Anyhow," Earl continued, "he wanted to buy a salve for a cut on his arm. Said it was a little worse than he thought. So I helped him out there. But then he proposed an idea to me, that I come out to this rally of his where there would be a whole lot of customers just waiting to be served, all in one place! How could I pass that up?"

"But what did he want in return?" asked John.

"He said he just wanted me to deliver messages from time to time in the next few weeks, since I travel so much. He said he had plans to send messages of meetings and so on."

"Didn't you want to know what the messages were about?" asked Ed.

"No," he said quietly. "The truth is I didn't, and I didn't ask to know, either. I guess deep down I knew this fellow was up to no good. I even told you so at the funeral."

"But you didn't know who Mr. Dupont really was, right?" asked John.

"No, that's true," said Earl. "But I ended up getting involved anyway…and nearly ended up getting in trouble myself by being there," he concluded. "Guess at my age I should know better."

"So, why were you up on that stage then?" asked John.

"Because he told me in Langham that I could be first to say a few words to the crowd if I attended. I wanted to let them know what new products I had and where I'd be set up afterwards. I was ready to make a small fortune in one night, that's all. But he hogged the whole stage and then the crowd went crazy…then young John here jumped up and gave the best darned speech I've ever heard in all my days…"

John felt his face grow warmer.

"…and then…well, that maniac showed up, as you well know. It wasn't the best night for an old salesman, that's for certain. The company you keep says something important, that's for sure."

"Say!" added Earl, looking especially at John and Elmer. "Come here for a minute, boys."

Earl glided over to his carriage with his usual smoothness and reached into the back. He pulled out a stack of encyclopedias, the thirteen volumes of the Ridpath set he had told them about.

"I want you boys to have these. They're not much use to someone who already knows more about the world than he wants to know. Maybe they'll help you with your schooling or help pass the time this winter," he said.

"But don't touch my Saskatoon berries!" he added with a flourish. "Those are mine."

"Thanks, Mr. Wright!" said John enthusiastically.

"Look, Mother," added Elmer. "Our own encyclopedias!"

Mary beamed and thanked Earl for his generosity, telling him he should drop in next week because she just might need a few kitchen spices replenished.

***

As the Diefenbaker wagon travelled alongside the train station on its way out of Borden, Mary bumped William on the arm and discreetly pointed. William slowed the wagon and then stopped, only a few feet away from a woman who was surrounded by three large suitcases as she sat on the train platform bench. Gertrude's Schneider's long brown dress was wrinkled and worn and her hair, as always, was tied tightly into a bun.

From the west, an east-bound steam train sounded its powerful whistle, signalling that it was almost at Borden. Mary got out of the wagon and approached Gertrude, while everyone else waited.

Gertrude's face wore the same bleak mask ever since the last full moon, where, under its splendid light, her husband had been murdered.

"Gertrude, did you hear they captured the man who killed Hans?" asked Mary, gently approaching.

Silence.

"They got him, Gertrude. He won't hurt anyone again," Mary said.

Mary desperately wanted this to mean something, but Gertrude only stared at her. Didn't it mean something? The powerful steam whistle of the train began to sound louder as it got closer to the train station.

Gertrude finally nodded in understanding.

"Did Hans come back?" she asked in her limited English.

Mary was taken aback by the question. "No, no of course

not. No one can bring Hans back."

"That's right," she said calmly. "No one can bring Hans back. Good bye, Mary." Gertrude placed her cold hand on Mary's briefly and squeezed it.

Before Mary could reply the steam whistle belched its great sounds into the morning air again, as the train pulled up and stopped at Borden's station. Mary gave her a stiff hug. She also wanted to say something else, but bit her tongue. Mary walked briskly towards the wagon with the realization that Gertrude had really left the Canadian West days ago under the light of the full moon.

A man loaded her suitcases into a train car. Mary saw only Gertrude's back as she boarded the train. She tried to picture the older woman in her beloved Germany, living out the rest of her life with memories of happier days.

***

At the Diefenbaker homestead, morning broke with quiet promise. The red sun leaked above the horizon, spreading mythic fires of red, gold and orange. Bathed in this light, its rough edges smoothed by nature's deft hand, the homestead seemed nearly an oasis to John after recent events.

As he milked the cows, John reflected on how much he already missed Summer, even though it had only been a day and a half since she went back to the reservation. He looked through the barn door opening and could see Prairie Dancer grazing with Blue and Skipper. She still had to come back for her horse, he thought happily. As well, she was usually able to visit during the harvest, which would begin in about two weeks. Soon the work crews would be here, too, making it the busiest time of year.

As he milked, John could hear something faint in the background, but it wasn't clear to him what the distant sound was.

"John!" called his father. "Come out here!"

John knew that his father and uncle were still working on the well while his mother and brother worked on gathering eggs and cleaning out the chicken coop. He wondered what all the excitement could be about. He set his milk pail down and quickly walked out of the barn. In the distance, a large dust cloud was moving closer and in the centre of it was a burst of horses that seemed to be charging toward the Diefenbaker homestead.

"What's going on?" asked John nervously. Elmer had already come out of the chicken coop and was staring, too.

"I'm not sure," said William, getting a better grip on the tool he was carrying. "Who are they, Ed?"

Ed squinted. "They're Indian, I think. But what tribe? Whoever they are, there're about forty of them…and they're picking up speed."

"Land sakes," said Mary, who was nervous because of the shouting.

As the broncos approached, the Diefenbakers steeled themselves for the unknown.

"Hey!" said John. "Isn't that Chief Five Hawk's headdress?"

Elmer agreed. "Yes! It's the Cree! And there's Summer... with her father!"

Just before the Cree reached the homestead they fanned out and surrounded the Diefenbakers in dramatic fashion, shouting the entire time. To the left of Chief Five Hawks was River's Voice and Summer riding together on the same horse, since Prairie Dancer was still with the Diefenbakers. When they came to a stop, William stepped forward.

"Welcome, Chief Five Hawks," said William, still not sure what was going on.

"Thank you, William Diefenbaker. We ride in big numbers today to honour you and your family."

Chief Five Hawks dismounted, as did River's Voice, who could not have looked more jubilant. All the other riders remained on their horses, their faces satisfied looking and fixed on the Diefenbakers in knowing smiles.

River's Voice spoke next.

"I would still be in jail if not for your family, William," he said, shaking his hand firmly. "I will never forget your family's kindness to me. Never, ever."

"We knew you couldn't have done what they said," said William truthfully. "I have to say, John here led the way in doing something about it."

John grinned shyly, realizing he wasn't exactly acting like the self-assured speech-maker who captivated a large audience and prevented a riot only two nights ago.

"I had a lot of help from my brother and Summer," said John honestly.

"We appreciate what all of you did," said River's Voice to everyone, smiling at Elmer, Mary, William, and Ed, too. "But it was you, John Diefenbaker, who had courage to push the police to re-think things. Without you, without a belief in the truth from you, I would not be with my daughter right now. I would not be with my band." He bowed briefly to John, shook his hand, and then stepped back to let Chief Five Hawks speak.

"You gave River's Voice the gift of freedom, John Diefenbaker. And it is an old Cree custom to honour the giver with a gift just as good or greater," said the old chief.

"But freedom has no equal, no greater, so what can I do? What can an old chief do?" he asked with wry smile, stroking his chin.

"What I can do, then," Chief Five Hawks answered himself, "is make you a chief, too."

Chief Five Hawks motioned John forward and Mary gave him a small push at the centre of his back so his feet would begin to work.

Chief Five Hawks placed a hand on John's shoulder. "Among us you are now Chief Thunder Eagle, for defending freedom and truth. May you always see clearly, John Diefenbaker. May you always have sight like the great eagle."

Chief Five Hawks added one more thought.

"May others one day benefit from this sight."

John looked back at his father who beamed with pride.

"I'm honoured, Chief Five Hawks. Thank you very much," said John.

"John Diefenbaker!" yelled River's Voice in a powerful voice with his fist raised in the air.

"John Diefenbaker!" everyone yelled at once, following suit, as all of the horses and riders began to shift and move with excitement.

Elmer let out an unrestrained whoop of joy for the honour his big brother received.

"To John Dief! Our best chief! Hey, Dief the Chief!" Elmer yelled.

Everyone laughed while Mary sized up her eldest son.

"Around this homestead, chiefs still milk their cows and clean up chicken coops, just so you know."

"Yes, Mother," said John smiling.

"I am a Canadian,
free to speak without fear,
free to worship in my own way,
free to stand for what I think right,
free to oppose what I believe wrong,
or free to choose those
who shall govern my country.
This heritage of freedom
I pledge to uphold
for myself and all mankind."

From the Canadian Bill of Rights,
July 1, 1960

Adopted by Prime Minister John Diefenbaker

A NOTE TO THE READER

Truth and Authenticity in
The Mystery of the Moonlight Murder

DON'T READ ON IF YOU HAVEN'T READ THE BOOK! SPOILER ALERT!

Although *The Mystery of the Moonlight Murder* is a work of fiction, there are many authentic themes, aspects, and details that I have tried to capture in the work. This is a brief commentary on these details and the list is by no means comprehensive.

All family names and personalities mentioned are as accurate as possible. This extends beyond the nuclear family even to other mentioned names. For instance, William's brother Duncan really did send the family apples from Ontario from time to time. Henry Diefenbaker actually did visit from Waukegan, Illinois earlier that summer. The reference to John and his Uncle Ed nearly freezing to death in a blizzard the previous winter is also accurate.

All of the historical discussions are accurate. As an example, the details of the rebellion as explained by Sergeant English and the Diefenbaker's comments are all true.

Section Eight, Township 418, was the actual homestead of the Diefenbaker family.The water well was a constant problem for the Diefenbakers. Having access to clean water was an ongoing struggle for them. A doctor really did tell William he should move out West for his health.

The sleeping arrangements for the Diefenbakers were just as described, with John at his Uncle Ed's and Elmer sleeping in his parents' kitchen.

The Long River Band is a made-up name for Summer's Cree band, as was its proximity to the Diefenbaker homestead. However, many steps were taken to ensure the Plains Cree lifestyle was accurately reflected, from language to customs, such as the naming ceremony.

Little touches were added, such as ensuring the song *All in Jesus* was real, and that it was a hymn written before 1908, when the story takes place. The advent of the telephone was very new in Saskatchewan at this time, with only a few hundred households owning the technology.

Some things were added that were adapted from John Diefenbaker's invaluable memoirs. For instance, he observed Indians catching rabbits by hand. In a flashback, John's thoughts are of young Summer Storm catching the rabbit with bare hands.

The distance between the village of Borden and the Diefenbaker homestead is a reasonable approximation.

American whisky smugglers really were a problem.

Summer Storm is fictional, as are all the other First Nation characters. However, their involvement in the story was meant to represent the importance John Diefenbaker ascribed to First Nations peoples. In his years as prime minister, Diefenbaker would extend the right to vote to First Nations people and received many honours from various First Nations chiefs. He also appointed James Gladstone to the Senate, the first Aboriginal Canadian ever appointed to the upper chamber.

When John asks his father about whether or not there is monetary help for the character of Gertrude once her husband dies, his father tells him that no such a thing exists. In the story he finds this unfair. Creating widow's pensions is something John Diefenbaker would one day address when he became prime minister.

The dream John has of the eagle, the buffalo on two legs and the many spotted horses were meant to symbolize some of the actual honours given to the former prime minister by First Nations peoples.

A prairie fire nearly did destroy the Diefenbaker homestead and it was saved by ploughing furrows around the home.

When Chief Five Hawks reflects on what the Queen Mother promised, these are direct quotes from Cree author, Joseph F. Dion, in his book My Tribe, the Crees. The author is describing an occurrence at Fort Pitt through an interpreter.

John and Elmer were forbidden to swim in the North Saskatchewan River and neither boy was a good swimmer. However, their ability with horses was strong and both were able to ride bareback.

The idea of the prisoner escape from the train is also based on a real pioneer story. I got the idea from a book that featured actual Canadian prairie homesteaders reminiscing about their memories of this time. One man recalled asking the train's engineer whenever it stopped in the evening "Got any tonight, mister?" referring to prisoners. Although he did not mention any escapes, this provided the germ of idea for that scene.

Mary really did sell butter in Rosthern, as the story mentions. By 1908, it is unclear whether or not she still did but it is a good guess that this means of extra family income continued. Langham was simply chosen for its proximity to the storyline.

The Langham Bruderthaler Mennonite Church was built before 1908. It still stands to this day.

We don't know of any experiences John Diefenbaker may or may not have had with black immigrants in the Canadian West. I thought it important to acknowledge their settlement story through a cameo appearance of a character that ends up playing a pivotal role in the capture of a criminal in the book. The young man, Matthew Carver, hails from Rosetown, Saskatchewan which really was one of the larger settlements of black Canadians in the west at this time.

Bellevue was a real Métis community.

There is an inside joke in Chapter 15. Sergeant English says that even Cyrus Ramsey's own defence lawyer will not represent him because it went against his principles. The reporter learns that the lawyer was named Arthur Meighen. Meighen, Canada's ninth prime minister, was actually a Winnipeg defence lawyer in 1908 when this story takes place. Meighen was known for his integrity and since I am also the author of Arthur Meighen: The Ferocious Debater Who Stuck to His Principles, I thought it would be amusing to bring him into the story-line.

In John Diefenbaker's memoirs, he talks fondly of the family owning a broken set of Ridpath Encyclopedias. I thought it would be interesting to suggest how the family acquired them.

Chief Five Hawks honours John with the title Chief Thunder Eagle. This is actually one of the honourary titles John accepted in real life, although after he became prime minister. Some of the other titles were Chief Many Spotted Horses and Chief Walking Buffalo, the symbols from his dream.

For nicknames as prime minister, John Diefenbaker actually did become known as The Chief, or Dief the Chief.

REFERENCES

Diefenbaker, John G., *One Canada: Memoirs of the Right* Honourable John G. Diefenbaker, Scarborough, Signet. 1978

Dion, Joesph F., *My Tribe, the Crees*, Calgary, Glen Bow Museum. 1979, p. 76-77

McNeil, Bill, *Voice of the Pioneer*, Toronto, Macmillan. 1978

TEACHERS!
VISIT WWW.RODERICKBENNS.COM FOR TEACHING WITH HISTORICAL FICTION AND A LIST OF PRIME MINISTER JOHN DIEFENBAKER'S KEY ACCOMPLISHMENTS.

About the AUTHOR

Born and raised in the scenic Kawartha Lakes area of Ontario, Roderick Benns has had a varied writing career spanning 18 years. He is the author of *Arthur Meighen: The Ferocious Debater Who Stuck to His Principles*, part of the Warts & All Prime Ministers series by JackFruit Press. Roderick is an award-winning journalist, having captured a first place national newspaper award in the 1990s for journalistic initiative through the Canadian Community of Newspapers Association. He is currently Senior Writer with the Literacy and Numeracy Secretariat of the Ontario Ministry of Education.

Family life is integral to Roderick. He is married to his wonderful wife, Joli Benns. Roderick has two magnificent children, Eric, and Alexis. They live in the Greater Toronto Area with their silver toy poodle, Sirius. The family also likes to spend time in the country with their young horse, Gaelin.

SUPPORT THE **LEADERS AND LEGACIES** SERIES...
Our People, Our Stories, Our Canada

"One wonders whether Canadians will possess a common national memory a generation from now given that three-quarters of high school graduates were unable to give the date of Confederation - a ten percent point decline in ten short years."
— Rudyard Griffiths, 2007,
The Dominion Institute

No matter how strong our regional roots are, it is our national identity that binds us together to form our common ground as Canadians. Leaders and Legacies is more than a book series - it is an opportunity to be part of a quiet, simple grassroots movement that aims to strengthen our national identity. It is a way to preserve and reinforce our common memory.

In reflection, the creation of Canada in 1867 was an improbability on many fronts, from its linguistic tensions to its small, disjointed population. On a vast scale it was not much more than a northern dream. And yet we Canadians, as diverse as we are, are connected by more than political will. Although we are unified through shared landscapes and political ties we are even more connected by our shared freedom to dream.

Leaders and Legacies aims to help children connect with leadership themes through the excitement of historical adventures.

CONSIDER GIVING THIS BOOK AS A GIFT TO A YOUNG PERSON YOU KNOW

Spread the Word!

• Buy a copy of this book at <u>firesidepublishinghouse.com</u> for your children, grandchildren or as a gift idea. **When you buy from Fireside, each book is personally signed by the author.**

• Canada needs more voices to support our national identity and our national stories. If you share news on a blog, forum or a website, share your thoughts about the idea of the Leaders and Legacies series. **Write a book review** for your local newspaper or for a favourite website.

• Store and business owners -- consider **displaying** this book on your counter or in some other available space. We offer discount pricing for purchasing six or more books.

• Contact the author and have him speak to your **group, class or service club** on the Prime Ministers and other aspects of Canadian history.

• If you want to read more about Canada's history visit www.roderickbenns.com and sign up for the **free newsletter**, The Canadian.